After three years and two months, Mr. Fisk was ready to love once more. And it was time for Fran to find a mother. Time for Clementine to have a gentleman upon her arm, and time for Miss Wiskerton to have her own Mr. Darcy.

Actually, it was time for *me* to intervene in these matters.

OTHER EGMONT USA BOOKS YOU MAY ENJOY

Callie's Rules
by Naomi Zucker

Frozen in Time
by Ali Sparkes

Leaving the Bellweathers
by Kristin Clark Venuti

Meanicures
by Catherine Clark

SCONES and Sensibility

lindsay eland

EGMONT
USA
NEW YORK

To my kiddos: Gracie, Isaac, Ella Jane, and Noah,
who make every day a dream come true.

And always, to John, who is my own Gilbert Blythe,
my real life Mr. Darcy, and the love of my life.

EGMONT

We bring stories to life

First published by Egmont USA, 2010
This paperback edition published by Egmont USA, 2011
443 Park Avenue South, Suite 806
New York, NY 10016

1 3 5 7 9 8 6 4 2

www.egmontusa.com · www.lindsayeland.com

THE LIBRARY OF CONGRESS HAS CATALOGED THE HARDCOVER EDITION AS FOLLOWS:
Eland, Lindsay.
Scones and sensibility / Lindsay Eland.
p. cm.
Summary: In a small New Jersey beach town, twelve-year-old Polly Madassa, who speaks like a character in her two favorite novels, "Pride and Prejudice" and "Anne of Green Gables," spends the summer making deliveries for her parents' bakery and playing matchmaker, with disastrous results.
ISBN 978-1-60684-025-2 (hardcover) — ISBN 978-1-60684-067-2 (reinforced library binding) [1. Dating services—Fiction. 2. Humorous stories.] I. Title.
PZ7.E355Sc 2009
[Fic]—dc22
2009018118

Paperback ISBN 978-1-60684-158-7

Book design by Jeanine Henderson

Printed in the United States of America

CPSIA tracking label information:
Random House Production · 1745 Broadway · New York, NY 10019

Contents

chapter one

In Which My Family Is Introduced and I Contemplate the Less-Than-Desirable Traits of My Dear Sister's Boyfriend

It was upon turning the last delicate page of my leather-bound copy of *Pride and Prejudice* that my transformation into a delicate lady of quality was complete.

Indeed, I had always been a romantic, and those dearest to me—my parents, whose love was like that in a fairy tale; my elder sister, Clementine; and my bosom friend, Fran Fisk, who I have known since preschool—can attest to this fact.

Tea parties with cucumber sandwiches had been my activity of choice since I was but a child of five. Most of my clothing from the time I took a breath in this world bore lace and ruffles (except during the unfortunate camping trip where I was forced into cutoff jeans and a tank top that bore the word WHASSUP?).

And in the fourth grade, after reading *Anne of Green Gables*, I formed a club with my dearest Fran and for months we reenacted the scenes from that most beloved book. But Fran was not nearly as entranced by the story as I was and became tired of watching me float down the river on her hot-pink raft whispering the verses to "The Lady of Shalott."

But we were friends born for each other's confidence and no amount of Lady of Shalott could tear us asunder.

So I do not think that Fran was surprised when I finished *Pride and Prejudice* just three months ago and announced that I would no longer remain a material girl living in a material world, but would rather grasp on to the skirts of those elegant women before me and become at once a young lady of impeccable breeding, diction, and manner.

Thus it was, as I reclined in my bedroom contemplating these things, that I was suddenly overcome with the summer's brilliance and glory. The air was thick and sweet like a newly blossomed hydrangea, and the smell of the salt water hanging on to the breeze like clothes pinned delicately on a line was intoxicating.

On most summer morns I woke to the enticing aro-

mas of fresh-baked bagels, pastries, and croissants. My parents, my sister, and I lived above our quaint bakery (what could be more romantic?!) just a stroll away from the boardwalk and the wild open sea.

I will say it once more: on *most* mornings.

As I sat up on that first day of summer, however, I knew my dearest elder sister had been in charge of the baking because the scent of burnt sugar swept under my door and overtook the breeze that blew in gentle and calm from my open window.

From below she stirred up a batter of cusswords that caused me to blush. It was definitely not the way any lady should behave, but my sister was a modern sixteen-year-old, whereas I, as my parents often stated, had become a "twelve-year-old, nineteenth-century girl trapped in the twenty-first century."

And of this, I assure you, I am most proud.

A gray stream of smoke poured under my doorway. "One," I counted, slipping out of my white linen night-gown and putting on my favorite summer dress—the one with the blue gingham pattern and the delicate ruffles along the collar. "Two." I heard Mama's soft footsteps coming from her room as she made her way down the stairwell. "Three," I said, just as the smoke alarm went off and another string of profanity wafted along with the smoke up through the grate and into my bedroom.

The burnt pastries and muffins, the charred bagels and breads. It was all inevitable when Clementine worked the morning bake shift, so I knew there was no reason for alarm. Instead, I exited my room with the white embroidered handkerchief my bosom friend Fran had given me for my birthday pressed against my nose. The smoke alarm blared above my head, so I delicately stepped up onto the stool I kept close for occasions such as these and waved my handkerchief back and forth until the abominable beeping ceased.

"This stupid oven burns everything!" I heard Clementine lament from below. "Everything!"

I sighed. My dear sister and I were but four years apart, but the distance seemed to have grown between us since she had reached the ripe age of sixteen. In our younger years, the two of us, our windblown curls streaming behind us, would spend hours together during the long, sun-kissed summers. Indeed, our beloved pastimes included: collecting seashells together, embarking on bicycle rides down to the local corner store, and spending the rainy days creating dainty bracelets and necklaces or improving our artistic eye with painting and drawing.

I lingered on the stairs, sighing over these memories. Indeed, I wished that once more the two of us would be entwined in sisterly affection and she would cease the habits that had become increasingly irritating as of late. Habits such as speaking for hours on the telephone with any number of boys (note that I do not call them gentlemen) and listening to blaring music much too loud for the entire household to bear, let alone for her to hear my remarks on propriety. And never having any time for the sister she had both loved and adored since birth.

Downstairs, Mama comforted Clementine, her tan arm wrapped around my sister's shoulders, which were splattered with flour and powdered sugar.

Papa walked in through the door with a bouquet of wildflowers in his hands.

"What's all this?" he asked, cradling my mother to his broad chest and kissing her lightly on the forehead. I walked over and hugged him around the waist and he gave me a small kiss on my alabaster cheek.

Clementine threw up her hands. "I've burnt the dumb pumpkin loaves again, that's what all this is!" A pout formed on her lips. Though self-control was not her strong point, and her temper was often painful to watch, her brow did curve downward in a very graceful arc when she was angered. I often attempted the same look in my mirror, but it never looked quite as regal. "And I told Clint to come by 'cause they're his favorite. Now what'll I give him?" I bit my tongue to stop the words that pushed to come out. Clint was my sister's newest boyfriend and one I heartily disapproved of.

His looks were pleasing to the eye, but beyond that his appeal lessened considerably. Not only had he made my lovely sister weep on numerous occasions, but never once had he given her flowers, opened her door, or given her any other tokens of affection that a woman desires from a suitor. He was a bore in my opinion and not nearly deserving of my darling sister. He insisted on referring to me as "Pol" and refused to allow me to join them on any of their evening walks, even though I could practically feel my sister's desperate yearning for me to join them pulsing in the air. He also insisted on addressing my parents by their given names: Judy (though her real name is Judith) and Sam (though his real name is Samuel).

I had desired the end of their connection practically before it commenced. Indeed, I often wished that I could find a more suitable beau for my dear Clementine. And seeing as I had such extensive knowledge on the subject of love and romance from my reading of Jane Austen, I was quite willing and prepared for the task.

The idea had merit, and I tucked it away for further contemplation.

"Not to worry, Clemmy," Papa said, taking the scorched loaves to the counter and wrapping each loaf in plastic wrap. "We'll sell them for a dollar each like we do the day-olds. We Madassas can fix anything. As for Clint, I bet he'd love one of our giant blueberry muffins."

The blackened loaves sat like large bricks in the wicker basket. In my opinion, it would have been better if they were completely incinerated in the oven rather than served to the waiting public. Really, I had no idea why Mama and Papa had given Clementine the task to begin with. "Your sister needs more responsibility, and besides we need the help during the busy summer season" is all Papa said when I had asked him the reason. But it didn't seem like things were busy enough to plunge the family business into financial hardship by letting Clementine attempt the morning baking. When I expressed this to him on another occasion, he replied, "You're being overly dramatic, Polly."

Of course, I had nothing against my beloved sister—

I loved her dearly as my own flesh and blood—but when you do not have a gift for baking, why force the matter?

"I know just how to soothe a disturbed and distressed spirit, my dearest sister. Come along and we shall frolic together among the salty waves of the sea! We shall bask in the sun's lovely rays," I said, reaching for her hand.

But Clementine turned toward me, her hands on her hips, with quite an exasperated look upon her face. "You're kidding, right, Polly? I don't have time for stupid stuff like that, especially when I burnt the stupid pumpkin bread and now I have to give Clint a stupid blueberry muffin."

My spirit sank low at her harsh choice of words, and hot tears threatened to cascade down my cheeks. "Well, you don't have to be so mean about it," I snapped back. "I was just trying to help. You're never any fun anymore!"

Mama wrapped her arms around me. "Thanks for trying, Polly. But it's not you, really, it's just . . . everything right now."

Clementine tore off her apron in a manner most unbecoming of a girl her age and flopped onto a nearby chair. "Stupid, stupid, stupid," she huffed most indignantly.

I smiled at my mother and attempted to arch my eyebrows in disapproval of my sister's behavior, but she had already turned her back on me and was busily lamenting the tragedies of the blackened bricks of bread, adding "stupid" to most every noun in her sentence.

So instead of lingering, I made my way into our small but sufficient family kitchen. There were day-old raspberry croissants sitting on the counter and I picked one up, nibbling the end as daintily as I imagined Miss Elizabeth Bennet would do. Now if only there was a bit of needlework about that needed to be completed—then I would be even more like that enchanting heroine.

But since there was none, I sighed, "Ah, me," and gazed out the window at the early-morning sun peeking its golden eye into the kitchen and kissing me with its tender rays. I closed my eyes and lifted my face to the heavens. Its beams soothed my recently rumpled spirit. "Indeed I know of no one that could not be at ease with the sun casting its smile upon the earth."

I slipped out the front door, hoping to go quite unnoticed by my family since this wondrous morning should not be spent in a bakery, no matter how quaint and romantic the bakery was.

I sat myself upon the lush grass and leaned back to

face the bright blue sky. There, I closed my eyes and imagined I was a wealthy maiden cast out of her family's castle for falling in love with a stableboy named *Free*-drick (for I much preferred this pronunciation to the ordinary Fred-rick). Here, in the Meadow of Wandering Dreams, he was to meet me.

"But what is taking him so long?" I wondered aloud.

The screen door creaked open behind me and I heard Clementine's voice. "Polly, what are you doing?"

I sat up and turned to her. "Oh Clementine, I am just soaking in the rays of love and life!" I stood up and reached out my hand. "Will you not take a turn with me out in the sunshine?" I twirled my way toward her, my dress billowing out around me like flower petals.

She rolled her eyes. "Polly, you're acting ridiculous. And you better come and help me or Mom'll have your head. The morning rush is starting and you're out here blabbering on about God knows what."

I sighed and I resigned myself to the task at hand. "Mama said that I only have to help with the bakery duties twice a week, dear Clementine. This will be my second time, so, yes, I shall be there momentarily."

"Whatever, Polly."

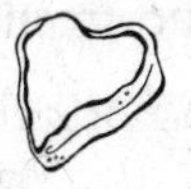

chapter two

In Which I Act as Patroness of the Bakery and I Suspect Discontent in My Bosom Friend

In the midst of the busy bakery I was able to tend to our beloved customers despite the glories of sunshine, flowers, and the wild ocean wind that beckoned from outside. Indeed, we had quite a number of loyal customers and it was always a joy to serve them.

"And what may I get for you this exquisite morning, Mrs. Sanders?"

The young woman smiled, a pretty dimple sitting quite happily in her right cheek. Ah, I had wished upon all things that I had been born with a dimple, but alas, I was not. And no amount of biting my cheek or drawing one on my face with a pen had sufficed. "The usual, if you have any left," she replied.

I smiled and examined our bakery case for the delectable cinnamon streusel muffin she adored so much and retrieved one from the case and placed it on a plate. "Indeed I do. It's the last one and I am so glad it is yours."

Mrs. Sanders was a good-natured woman of thirty-six who had recently moved to our fair town with her husband to assist with his aging mother, and had visited us most mornings since her arrival. She was a pleasant woman, though shy in manner.

I then assisted Miss Morgan, who was quite taken with the buttercream muffin, five people whose names were unknown to me and who had a certain fetish for our walnut Danish, and Mr. Lampert, who was making his way down our menu and ordered the quite scrumptious chocolate chip Danish.

And then there was Clint, who entered our sophisticated bakery like a great boorish beast and leaned on the counter. "Hey, Pol. Clemmy said she'd make me some pumpkin loaves this morning."

I arched an eyebrow at him and lifted my nose into the air at his behavior.

But before I could utter a word, Clementine, who had left me momentarily to bring out more clean dishes, came through the door.

"Hey, Clint," she said, her cheeks blushing to a rosy hue. "I'm glad you came."

He smiled and leaned over, his arms practically lying across the counter. "Hey, can you take a break and eat with me?"

Clementine looked upon me and smiled. "I'll just be a few minutes, Polly," she said, taking off her apron and coming from behind the counter before I could make any protestation. "Thanks!"

"Indeed!" I stated, and watched them with extreme disapproval as they found a seat and began whispering together.

After assisting two other customers, I determined to put an end to Clint and Clementine's rendezvous. It was my duty as a sister to aid her.

So unwrapping one of the hardened pumpkin loaves, which could be likened now to a lump of coal, I took up a plate and walked over to the table where they sat in deepest conversation. Then, placing the plate down rather hard upon the table, I dumped the loaf onto the plate, where it most likely cracked the white porcelain. "Here's your pumpkin loaf, Clint. Clemmy made them extra hard just for you. Now come along with me, Clementine. You must assist me behind the counter."

Clementine glared at me quite viciously, but I chose to ignore it, for I knew that in saving her from further conversation with this horrible boy, I was in the right.

And as Clementine and I continued to assist customers, I found enjoyment in watching Clint attempt to eat the loaf, which I knew to be quite impossible. After having spent some time gnawing on the blackened crust, he gave up and rejoined Clementine at the counter. "You might need to work on those loaves, Clemmy," I heard him say. "I almost broke a tooth biting into it." And then thankfully he left the bakery and the sun seemed to shine once more.

"Humph," I said. "Perhaps tomorrow we may be so lucky that he will indeed break a tooth. But one can only hope."

"Can it, Polly," Clementine huffed, and left me to attend to the other waiting customers.

The morning continued on, and in between tending to our patrons, I was able to reread little snippets of *Pride and Prejudice* and relish in the words and romance that leapt off the page at me.

Indeed I was so enraptured by the scene where Miss Elizabeth Bennet meets Mr. Darcy for the first time that I did not notice my bosom friend enter with her beloved father, Mr. Fisk.

"Hey, Polly!" Fran said, startling me to the present.

I placed the book upon the counter and grasped her hands in mine, noticing a brand-new friendship bracelet encircling her delicate wrist. Indeed, Fran enjoyed making these bracelets more than any other activity, it seemed. She had even recently declared that she hoped to be a jeweler when she grew up, which I thought very romantic indeed.

"Hey, Fran! I mean . . . why dearest Fran, Mr. Fisk. What a pleasant surprise to find you in our midst!"

Mr. Fisk smiled. "I've been craving one of your cinnamon rolls and coffee for the past few days. And well, Fran and me get a bit . . . lonely sometimes bumping around our house with just the two of us. So I said, 'what the heck,' turned off my computer, and here we are."

"Well, it is wonderful indeed!" I proclaimed, though I was quite alarmed at Mr. Fisk's use of the word *lonely*. He had never used such a word before. Though I must admit I had yearned to hear just such a sentiment.

Three years ago my best friend and her beloved father found out that Mrs. Fisk had fallen deeply and completely in love with a man she had met on the computer.

No one had heard from her since.

Were he and my dearest friend really. . . lonely? The thought was disconcerting, though a part of me thrilled at what exactly that could mean for my bosom friend and her father. What I *hoped* it could mean.

"I guess I'll have a cinnamon roll, too," Fran said.

I smiled and attempted to read her face that did, in fact, appear a bit forlorn, and dare I say. . . lonely? My heart ached for her! "But of course. And you and your father will receive nothing but the royal treatment at Madassa Bakery. So please, take a seat and I'll have it right out to you."

And as they made their way to a small table big enough for three or four people, which seemed to quite swallow them up, I could not help but watch them closely for any appearance of the said loneliness and despair (which in books often go hand in hand).

I imagined my dear friends alone in their house on a cold, snowy winter's morn. The snow outside keeping them indoors and the light of the fire casting shadows about the near-empty living room. Together they sat, though not a word was spoken.

Then I thought of the two of them sitting at their breakfast table, both lost in their own worlds of loneliness, and quietness being their constant companion.

Poor Fran. And poor Mr. Fisk.

The horrible news of Mrs. Fisk came as a shock to Fran, who was a mere child of nine, as well as to her father, who at the time was forty-two and had no idea how to make any meal besides cold cereal. Indeed, up until a few months prior, that is the only nourishment that my dearest bosom friend received, besides the occasional manufactured chicken nugget.

Fran came through the unfortunate computer-dating incident relatively unscathed, though I cannot say the same for her father. Mr. Fisk, who is practically my second father, has spent most of the past three and a half years cooped up in his office with his loathsome computer or on his way to his office to spend time on his loathsome computer.

Either way, his behavior was highly unhealthy.

The shock of Mrs. Fisk hit me hard as well. I had known the woman as a devoted, elegant mother who adored her husband, daughter, and myself with all of her heart and soul. When she departed, I mourned deeply for my wounded friend.

But even more, I wept at the loss of romance and the splintering of a marriage I had imagined would continue throughout eternity. Indeed, I knew that I would never have to endure the hardship of losing a parent to an online suitor, since my own dear father and mother have a love that is one of those found only in such romances as my dearest Jane Austen or Lucy Maud Montgomery have written. But still, something was lost in the moment Mrs. Fisk left and I have attempted over these past three years to regain the hope of true love once more. And indeed it was reading *Anne of Green Gables* and *Pride and Prejudice* that slowly healed the wound and gave me hope once more for my bosom friend and her father.

And yet now Mr. Fisk had spoken the sorrow-laden word *lonely* and Fran looked every bit the part of a despairing girl. Indeed, Mr. Fisk had been quite jovial the past few months, and had obviously decided that brushing his hair and wearing something other than sweatpants was not an unforgivable sin. I gazed at his person and nodded at the way his hair was combed quite nicely to the side, and his button-up shirt looked very handsome, if not a tad on the wrinkled side.

Could it be that Mr. Fisk was indeed ready for love once more? Could it be that Fran was in desperate want of a mother?

My heart thumped in my chest at the wondrous yet terrifying thought. Hope that was but a seed in my soul sprouted its promise inside me.

And perhaps I, Polly Madassa, could also take my

dearest friends under my matchmaking wing? Excitement bubbled inside me at the thrill of possibly bringing true love to my dearest friends.

Imagine. Mr. Fisk's arm wrapped around the slender waist of a most elegant woman called Cordelia Amaryllis. Fran holding her hand and calling her "beloved stepmother."

Yet the word *stepmother* conjured up images and thoughts that were not very pleasant. My dearest friend sent off to boarding school and forced to live in a dark attic with nothing but cobwebs and a lump of coal to soothe her. Or even worse, Fran living in her own house but considered a servant; forced to clean a very dirty chimney—her once rosy cheeks soiled by the soot and ash of disgrace. Cinder-Fran. The name was as vile as the images they projected!

I shook the visions from my head and imagined a kind stepmother. For certainly there were many kind ones present in the world—I was convinced upon it. She and Fran sewing by candlelight, or perhaps walking along the beach collecting seashells.

"Polly Madassa, what in the world are you doing?"

I jumped from out of my reverie and found Mama and Papa standing before me, gazing at the brown puddle on the floor. Indeed, I had become so engrossed in the misfortunes of my dearest friends that I had quite filled up Mr. Fisk's coffee a few times over, and it was now dripping onto the floor. "Oh my gosh! I'm so sorry," I said, reaching for a towel and sopping up the coffee. "I just got caught up in thinking of Fran and Mr. Fisk and Cordelia Amaryllis."

"And I suppose these were supposed to be cinnamon rolls?" Mama said. Indeed, much could not be said for the cinnamon rolls I had placed in the oven to merely warm. They were both quite charred (though please note that they were not nearly as blackened as the unfortunate pumpkin loaves of earlier) and the sugar now scorched the bottom of the oven, from which smoke was beginning to billow.

Clementine peeked over my father's shoulder and arched her eyebrow at me. "See, I told you that oven burns everything."

chapter three

In Which I Deliver Dog Bones to a Vile Dog and Come to the Aid of My Bosom Friends

I let out a sigh as Mama locked the front door precisely at 1:00 and turned over our sign announcing that Madassa Bakery was now closed. Indeed, I had just finished cleaning the oven and was quite dismayed at the fact that I was not able to serve Fran and her father. Papa had insisted that he take care of them while I slaved over the unfortunate mess.

Fran and dear Mr. Fisk left the bakery hours earlier with nothing but a wave and an "I'll call you later, Polly, okay?"

"This is most vexing to me," I said aloud. (I had learned the word *vexing* from dear Jane Austen and had hoped to find a circumstance in which I could use it. This was definitely one such moment.) "Yes, I am very vexed indeed," I said again.

My dearest bosom friend and her father were perhaps about to embark on the most wondrous journey of finding a companion and loving stepmother and I was unable to speak with them or even study them because I was sentenced to cleaning up the unfortunate coffee spill and cinnamon roll burning. And it was I who needed to help Mr. Fisk find his Elizabeth Bennet.

"Vexing."

Not to mention that dearest Clementine was still quite vexed with me for disrupting her rendezvous with Clint earlier.

"Very, very vexing," I said, enjoying the sound that the words made. Indeed, it sounded just like how I felt at the moment.

"Thanks, Polly," Papa said, placing a kind hand upon my shoulder. "It was a busy morning."

I looked up from my thoughts, nodded in agreement, and gazed at the shelves empty of all but the unfortunate pumpkin loaves. "Indeed it was, Papa. And now I think I will take a small turn about the neighborhood, for I have much to contemplate and my spirit is much . . . vexed."

"Turn about the neighborhood?" Mama asked, removing her apron.

Papa laughed. "I think she's going on a walk. Right, Polly?"

"Yes, Papa," I said, and I turned to leave.

"Well, if you're going on your 'turn' why don't you contemplate yourself down to Miss Wiskerton's and deliver these leftover bagels and some of these homemade dog bones for Jack. I think she gets pretty lonely all by herself, now that her mother has passed."

Though I wished to speak upon the subject of her temperamental dog and the fact that he was very undeserving of the bones, I kept my tongue quiet, took the bag from my mother's hand, and left the house quite a bit more vexed than before.

Yet the sun was successful in her cheer, and by the time I had walked a few steps I could not help but smile and find myself quite contented with my turn about the neighborhood as well as the delivery I was to make.

I strolled along the sidewalk toward Miss Wiskerton's cottage, enjoying the warmth of the sun and the fragrant sea salt hanging thick in the air, and thinking of the woman. Indeed, her story was quite tragic. An aging maid who had never known the romantic love of a gentleman, for she spent her every moment doting on her unwell mother. This had also turned her into quite a trollish figure, always in a state of agitation at something or someone.

A sorrowful story indeed.

I continued on my way and was stopped no more than fifty feet from said woman's house. Miss Eugenia May Wiskerton spent most days beached on her lawn chair with her disagreeable dog, Jack the Nipper (Fran and I had named him such after an unfortunate incident when he broke away from his restraint). Yet today was quite different.

The mailman, Mr. Snookers, was delivering the mail, much to Jack the Nipper's protest, and Miss Wiskerton seemed to be in quite a frenzy of excitement. At the same time she attempted to calm the ferocious beast, her cheeks flushed, and she kept trying to fluff up her hair, which sat in sausagelike rolls on her head.

Mama's voice came back to me at once: "I believe she is just a lonely maiden in need of love's kiss" or something quite similar.

I quickened my step to her small gate as Mr. Snookers ran past me at quite an astonishing speed when one considers his girth. Jack the Nipper was subdued as much as a dog of his disposition could be, and Miss Wiskerton appeared to look down the street at the retreated mailman with a hint of remorse.

Miss Wiskerton was indeed lonely. Lonely for love.

"Good day, Miss Wiskerton. I hope you are fine this morning?"

"Hello, Polly," she said, turning back to her lawn chair.

Jack the Nipper stared viciously at me with his blackened eyes, but I lifted my nose to him, unwilling to fall under his spell of intimidation. Still, I felt it unwise to enter the gate, lest my dainty ankles be punctured by his pointed, bloodthirsty teeth.

"I have brought you some of our famous bagels as well as some treats for Jack," I said, causing her to turn back around.

She smiled, and indeed it was a rather pretty smile, if not a little wrinkled by the sun. "Thank you, Polly. Jack loves those bones, and you know how I feel about the Madassa bagels."

I smiled, quite pleased with our family's reputation with the lady.

"But," she said, wagging her plump finger at me, "there was enough smoke billowing out of your house earlier today to kill a person on the spot. I guess these bagels are to pay me off so that I don't call the cops."

I shook my head, my curls dancing lightly around my shoulders. "Indeed not, Miss Wiskerton. I am afraid that Clementine was in charge of the morning baking and quite charred a few loaves of pumpkin bread."

Miss Wiskerton sat down on her chair and pulled out a bagel. "Well, I'd take her off the baking if I were you. She's sure to bring you all to ruin and set fire to the entire neighborhood while she's at it."

"I could not agree more, though my parents are quite determined that she learn how to bake." Indeed, she was in quite a trollish mood this morning and I desired to leave at once. "Well, I must be off. I hope you enjoy the bagels and have a most pleasant day."

The elegant lady huffed, then lifted a small book off the ground. I noticed its title immediately: *Persuasion,* by my own beloved Jane Austen! Though I had not read the book myself, any lover of that famed author was a dear friend of mine.

"Why, Miss Wiskerton. Do you enjoy the works of Jane Austen?"

The lady looked up at me and smiled, her harshness softening. "Yes, I do. I've read all her novels, though this is my favorite. What's yours?"

"Well, I have read only *Pride and Prejudice,* and I must say it is the dearest book to me."

"Yes, that was my mother's favorite, too. She had me read it to her every spring and never seemed to get tired of hearing it." Her voice caught on the last words, and she dabbed at her eyes. "I haven't been able to bring myself to read it again just yet."

Miss Wiskerton's obvious distress caused my heart to ache with sadness. And seeing that Jack the Nipper was temporarily absorbed in taking out his vicious aggression on one of Mama's bones, I stole inside the gate and stood by the dear woman's side.

"Well, be assured that if you would ever care to read it along with me, I'd be most delighted. It is sometimes trying on the soul to be speaking of Mr. Darcy to a group of people and no one around you truly understands how wonderful and noble the gentleman was."

She smiled. "I'd like that."

I reached down and squeezed her doughy hand in my own. "You know, dear Miss Wiskerton? I have always doubted the rumors that you were a mean and disgruntled old troll. Indeed, I suspected you were a kindred spirit all along. I'm so glad that it's mostly true."

Miss Wiskerton looked at me with surprise and then laughed quite heartily. "Well, thank you, Polly. At least I think."

I let go of her hand and curtsied. "Good day, Miss

Wiskerton. Enjoy your reading, as I am certain you will."

"All right, Polly, but still I'd talk to your parents if I were you. Surely they'll stop that sister of yours before she kills off the neighborhood."

"Indeed, I shall!" I called back to her. And at that I started off toward home, contemplating Miss Wiskerton's genuine loneliness, her deep yearning for a gentleman's company, and her love of Jane Austen.

It was fate!

I must find the woman her one true love, as well as Clementine and Mr. Fisk! Indeed, the three of them were all in desperate need of my help, though obviously they were not suited for each other.

No, each of them would require my special and unique attention. That is, if Mr. Fisk was ready for love. I needed to be certain of this before I began.

But I could feel it pulsing in the air around me! This indeed was going to be a summer filled with romance.

I swept into my home on the wings of this promise and immediately retired to my bedroom, where I read the first four chapters of *Pride and Prejudice* once more.

And I was so caught up in the words of dear Jane

Austen that I hardly heard the telephone ringing. "Hello, Madassa residence, Elizabeth Bennet speaking," I declared, and at once recognized my fault. "I mean, Polly speaking."

"Hey, Polly. Something's going on with my dad." It was my dearest Fran. I could hear distress in her voice. We were so closely entwined as friends that we knew each other's thoughts practically before they were spoken.

"Oh, dear Fran, whatever is the matter with your dearest father?" Though I did have my own suspicions, I withheld speaking them until I was more assured. Instead, I picked up a pen and began practicing the cursive letter *D* (for it was the one letter that gave me much trouble when I attempted to write it) over and over again on the small tablet of paper by my telephone.

"He's making chicken cordon bleu for dinner, *again*. And then," she lowered her voice, and I felt the urgency pulse across the telephone wires, "he made a raspberry torte for dessert . . . from scratch."

I was startled by this so entirely that I jumped slightly, causing an unsightly bump in the *D* I had been practicing.

Obviously, being the daughter of the owners of

Madassa Bakery, I know how long it takes to make a raspberry torte from scratch. Mr. Fisk would've had to spend at least two hours out of his office, something he hadn't done since he took Fran and me to New York City to see a show, and even then he'd brought along his laptop. This was highly alarming news.

"Really, a raspberry torte? Whoa. I mean . . . my gracious!"

"Polly, I just don't think I can eat the cordon bleu again. He's made it every single night for the past two months! It's like he's torturing me or something."

"I'm sure that is not the case, dearest Fran, for your father adores you. Still, this is very significant news."

"Well, what should I do? I mean, this is like the second month I've eaten that chicken thing for dinner and it would be nice to have a hamburger and French fries for once, like a normal person."

"Dearest Fran, there is no need to resort to that. Instead we must meet, for I think I may know what is troubling your father."

"Really? Well, at least someone has an idea. You wanna come over for dinner? We can talk and . . . it'd be nice to have someone else to eat with us."

"Indeed, Fran. Do you not like dining with your father?" Though I was suspicious earlier that she was lonely, I wondered if indeed she would declare it aloud!

"Well... of course I like having dinner with him, he's my dad. It's just that... with just the two of us all the time it still seems kind of... I don't know... weird."

"Really, it's weird? I mean, your father is most attentive and loving. I was unaware that you felt perturbed by regular meals together."

"Well, it can get kind of . . . lonely, I guess."

Could it be? Dare I hope? Oh, blessed afternoon! "Oh, Fran! This is most wonderful news!"

"It is? I said I was *lonely*, Polly. What's so wonderful about that? It's terrible. All alone all the time." At once I heard the pout in her voice and realized my faulty comment.

"Oh, yes, quite. I did not mean that. I do think we must meet, though."

"So do you wanna come for dinner, then?"

"Oh my gosh, yes!" I said, and then sighed with relief at her suggestion and composed myself properly. "It is a most welcome invitation, Fran. Indeed, I do not doubt my parents' consent and so will join you as soon as I am able to leave."

"All right, I'll see you in a bit."

"Farewell, my dear friend. And know that this, too,

shall pass and we together will right these wrongs! Adieu!" And I hung up the phone.

"Was that Fran?" I turned to find Mama standing in my doorway.

"Why yes, Mama. She has asked if I might join her and Mr. Fisk for dinner. It seems that the two of them are quite . . . *lonely*." I said this last word with much emphasis, though Mama seemed to overlook it.

She smiled. "That's fine by me. Have fun, and be back before nine."

I hugged her close to me. I said, "Thank you, Mama," and placed a kiss upon her rose-petal cheek and descended the stairs.

"Until tonight," I called out behind me, and, with the words of Jane Austen still on my tongue and the story close to my heart, I was off.

chapter four

In Which I Am Assured of My Friends' Loneliness and Have an Unfortunate Incident with Raspberry Cordial

The journey to Fran's cottage was a welcome one. As I bicycled along the streets I felt the wind rushing through my hair, and the ribbon I had tied to my sunbonnet streamed out behind me in a most elegant way.

Upon reaching her abode, I found Mr. Fisk sitting on the front step, sipping a small glass of lemonade.

"Good afternoon, dear Mr. Fisk," I said, dismounting with grace from my bicycle. Indeed it was a surprise to find him out in the fresh air enjoying a summer's day, so used was I to seeing him sitting inside his office.

My heart thrilled at the sight! Surely this was just another sign of his readiness to embrace love once more.

"Hi, Polly!" he called, patting the stair beside him.

"Is my dearest friend at home, Mr. Fisk?" I inquired.

"She'll be back in a bit. She's just picking up some sugar for us at the corner store. I used almost all of it to make a raspberry torte this morning."

"Ah yes, she spoke of this dessert to me earlier today." Though I wished Fran were here, I was thankful for the time with just me and her father since I could get a much better understanding of his readiness. "And what caused you to try such a delectable dish?"

He shrugged his shoulders, yet a smile crossed his face. "A friend I have on the Internet gave me the recipe, so I thought I'd give it a shot. I think it turned out pretty good."

"I am quite sure it did." We sat in silence for a moment, and I contemplated how to approach my next inquiry. It pained me to open the old wound of his former wife, but I knew I must if I was to know for sure that love was in his near future. "Mr. Fisk, may I ask you a quite delicate question?"

"Sure, Polly," he said. "We're good friends. Shoot."

"Well, I also was wounded deeply by Mrs. Fisk's departure three years ago. But having had time to heal with the help of Fran, my own dear parents,

Clementine, and of course, Jane Austen, I no longer feel anger toward her, and neither do I feel despair for love. Quite the contrary, I am quite hopeful with love."

He laughed very softly. "If you're wondering if I'm okay now, I am. As you know, I wasn't okay for a while, and I never wish that kind of hurt on anyone, but I'm good now . . . great even. I made it through, and you know, I'm better for it."

"And I know that your dearest daughter is healing from the wound as well. I try to be most attentive to her feelings on this subject."

At that moment Fran appeared from down the sidewalk, a small bag of sugar in her delicate hands.

Mr. Fisk patted me on the shoulder. "Thanks for asking about me, Polly. Fran has a good friend in you."

"You are most welcome," I said, and then joined Fran on the walkway. "My dearest friend, we have much to speak with each other about."

"All right, come on, Polly." And I followed her into the house and to her bedroom. "I just got some new embroidery thread to make some bracelets and also some nail polish."

"Oh, that sounds wonderful!" Indeed, though I enjoyed creating the bracelets with Fran, I did not like to actually wear them, but painting my dainty nails an elegant antique pink was highly appealing.

Still I could hardly think of doing either at such a time as this.

My heart was nearly bursting inside my chest at the thought of dear Mr. Fisk ready for love once more, which he clearly was. And though I was quite certain of it—was my dearest bosom friend ready for a new motherly confidante? Surely this woman could never replace the mother who had cradled Fran in her arms and had sung sweet lullabies over her sleeping babe. Yet still, I was almost sure that Fran did, indeed, desire a companion for her father as well as a mother to confide in.

I was in desperate need to know.

"So, beloved Fran. Please elaborate on what you were saying recently to me," I said with polite delicateness. I reached for the nail polish and cringed at the bright blue color. "You know, about being lonely."

Fran sighed and plopped onto her bed with little ceremony. "Well, it just gets weird the two of us all the time. It's like something's missing." She twirled a strand of golden hair around her finger. "Maybe we need a dog or a cat."

"Ah, Fran. I do not think that you need to go to such hairy extremes to find companionship." A vision of

Jack the Nipper gawking at me with his vicious teeth bared flitted through my mind and I pushed it away.

Instead, I turned my gaze away from her and smiled with elation. Indeed, you do not need to resort to that, dear friend! I imagined a beautiful woman brushing Fran's long blonde hair as she sat upon her bed, the woman placing a doting kiss upon my friend's noble brow and placing a delicate necklace around my friend's slender neck. "I wanted you to have this, Fran," the woman would say.

"Are you okay, Polly?"

I turned to find Fran looking at me with curiosity.

"Indeed, I am better than okay, dear Fran!" My heart could barely contain my happiness, though I managed to suppress my joy. "Being with you and your father is soothing to my very soul!"

"Well, I don't know how soothing it's going to be eating that stupid chicken cordon bleu for the millionth time. I mean really, Polly, what do you think is wrong with him?"

I allowed a small smile to grace my lips, yet I restrained myself from fully putting *everything* forth. "I believe I have found the reason for your father's sudden love of chicken cordon bleu and for his advancement into the raspberry torte. And indeed it is the most wondrous and happiest of reasons." I held up my hand to desist her from asking me questions. "But I cannot reveal my suspicions yet . . . not until I am quite sure of them."

"But Polly, he's my dad. I think I should have some idea of what you think might be wrong with him."

"Indeed, you are right, Fran. But I do not want to raise your hopes so high when it is merely a suspicion that I have." I reached for her hands and squeezed them. "I vow to reveal them as soon as I am more certain, and dear Fran, I suspect that will be very soon."

I could tell by Fran's face—the way her mouth formed an unsatisfied pout and her eyebrows narrowed at me—that she was not going to stop pestering me for all the world. Yet fate was on my side, for just then Mr. Fisk rapped lightly on the door. "Dinnertime, girls!" and I was saved from the unfortunate task of hiding my thoughts from my bosom friend.

"Oh, no," Fran lamented, holding her stomach as if in pain. "I just don't know if I'll be able to choke down another piece of that dinner."

I placed a loving arm around her, and together we descended the stairs to the kitchen. "Fear not, my friend. This, too, shall pass."

The meal was delicious, though I can attest to

my bosom friend's feelings that to have this meal—however delicious it may be—for two months straight would be a stretch for any palate. This excluded Mr. Fisk, who ate the meal with as much relish as if it were his first time, which did astonish me greatly.

My bosom friend sat across from me at the table, and throughout the meal I watched in horror as Fran spit out bite after bite of her chewed-up food into multiple napkins, so that at the end of the meal she had collected piles of wadded-up paper.

"Ready for dessert, you two?"

Fran was very excited, seeing as she received no nourishment at all during the meal. Her stomach, indeed, was most likely very hungry.

"It sounds delicious, Mr. Fisk," I said. "For there is hardly any fruit I know of that is as pure and romantic and elegant as the raspberry. And dear me, when you pair that with a torte, I think we shall all be in heaven."

He smiled, though I am not sure if he understood my meaning until Fran offered a translation. "She's really excited. Right, Polly?"

"Yes, very."

Fran helped her father in the kitchen while I was swept away in the romance of what this scene could be. My gaze fell on the empty chair that sat just opposite of Mr. Fisk. A chair void of any female person. Yet a chair that indeed longed for a . . . a . . . sitter (for lack of a better, more refined word). I imagined the woman, slender and beautiful, with merry eyes and a tender smile. In the vision, the woman offered a witty joke that delighted Mr. Fisk, Fran, and myself, their elegant dinner guest. Then once the meal was cleared away, we would all sit down together for a rousing game of whist, followed by a brisk walk along the ocean shores.

Ah yes. They would be a family like one from a book. Indeed, I was sure of it. This was what Mr. Fisk and my dearest friend were yearning for.

"All right," Mr. Fisk declared as he entered the dining room with a large plate. "I hope it tastes good."

The dessert was indeed delicious, if not a tad on the sugary side. And though Fran asked if I might stay the night, and I hated to leave her company, I politely declined.

"Dear Fran," I whispered, as we stood upon the porch. "I must go home and reflect a bit more on your father's situation. And I vow to call you on the morrow!"

We parted with a hug and the promise of meeting the next afternoon.

Once at my own home, I swept into the kitchen on a cloud of romantic thoughts. There was still much to contemplate and much to imagine before the night was through.

I would need refreshment while I was about the business of love.

Opening the refrigerator, I found nothing that could spark the imagination and nothing romantic enough to aid me in my quest.

Yet I found a dainty batch of frozen raspberries and, having just had a most magnificent torte at the Fisk home, was tempted beyond any resistance to make a glass of raspberry cordial for myself.

Indeed, I could think of nothing so romantic and inspirational than a tall glass of this elegant drink.

And so I set to the task, emptying the raspberries into a pot and adding a little more than a cup of sugar. Then, turning on the stove, I waited for the mixture to come to a simmering boil.

I sat upon a chair and sighed, my thoughts turning over the pleasant events of the evening and the love that Fran and her father would soon find.

Indeed, I was sure of my suspicions.

After three years and two months, Mr. Fisk was

ready to love once more. And it was time for Fran to find a mother. Time for Clementine to have a gentleman upon her arm, and time for Miss Wiskerton to have her own Mr. Darcy.

Actually, it was time for *me* to intervene in these matters.

Why must it be me?

Clementine was blind to all that Clint was, and Miss Wiskerton was still in the throes of pain from her mother's death. And then there were Mr. Fisk and Fran.

Mr. Fisk rarely left his office except to make the now-dreaded meal, and Fran was clearly too emotional about the whole situation to see things objectively. Besides, Fran had no other siblings to speak of besides a cat that came each evening for scraps or the dog they were forced to give away on account of its . . . its urinary tract problem.

I was the only one that could do the job.

Besides, I was good at all things having to do with the ways of love. I was probably one of the only ones who predicted in the opening chapters that Elizabeth would find Mr. Darcy in the end and that Anne Shirley would eventually become madly attached to one Gilbert Blythe. Matchmaking, specifically, happened to be my forte. I had introduced the Dalmatian down the street to the bulldog next door. Their relationship had been successful, ending in a litter of puppies that, though they were not much to look at, were adored by their parents.

This was my destiny!

I breathed in deep, sighing at the prospects before me, and was at once alarmed by the smell of smoke, and startled as the fire alarm blared above my head.

Mama burst into the kitchen. "Polly, what's going on now?"

I sprang from my chair and waved my hands in the air in an attempt to disperse the smoke that had quite filled the kitchen.

"I was going to make a glass of raspberry cordial," I said.

Once the scorched pot was placed into the sink, the windows opened to the outside, and the fire alarm stopped, Mama stood before me, her face a mystery all except for the touch of anger lingering in her eyes. I smiled and attempted to brush the soot from Mama's apron.

"Sorry," I said. "I was just so caught up in the prospects of love that I completely forgot about the delicious drink I was concocting."

"Polly, this is the second time today you've let your daydreams carry you away. And it's the third time that we've smoked out the house!" Mama ran her fingers through her hair, which I thought was unwise since it left behind a blackened residue upon her lovely blonde locks.

"I really didn't mean to. It's just that it's so easy to get swept away and I can't seem to help—"

Mama sighed. "Well, just make sure it's all cleaned up before you go to bed. And next time, if you think you might get swept away, *don't* turn on the oven or the stove."

"But that is partially the problem, Mama. And I'm sure you can remember being lost in your own imagination. I just never know when I might get taken away by the moment."

"Well then, we need to figure out something for you to do so that you aren't getting 'swept away' or the house is going to burn to the ground. But for now, since you never know when it'll happen, *never* turn on the stove. Problem solved." And she departed through the kitchen doors.

Indeed, it was disheartening that my romantic drink was ruined and my dearest Mama was once again upset. Yet I did not let this ruin my spirits.

Instead, as I wiped down the countertops and scrubbed the scorched pot, I thought of my best friend with her adoring stepmother—the two of them buying clothing, getting their hair done, making bracelets, and then the two of them creating a variety of foods together (none of which was chicken cordon bleu).

For everyone knows a girl cannot live on chicken cordon bleu alone.

chapter five

In Which I Am Burdened by a Job

"Polly," Mama said, an apron hugging her dainty middle. "Since Clementine will be doing the early-morning baking, I want you to do the delivering this summer. Your dad and I will pay you." She filled a brown paper bag with a dozen bagels of different variety, then stapled it shut. "And I hope that it'll keep your mind occupied enough that it won't get 'swept away' nearly as often, so we can save the house from burning down around us."

I closed my eyes and sighed. "I'm so sorry, Mama. But really, this is not a good summer to give me a delivery job, or any job for that matter. I have an important goal to be met in just three months. I'm really much too busy." I reached for her hands and squeezed them in my own. "It pains me to leave you in such a predicament but I'm sure there is a local high school urchin looking for a few extra farthings to get them through the summer." I turned to go but was stopped by her hand on my shoulder, digging a little too firmly into my ivory skin.

Mama smiled, holding the bag with our MADASSA BAKERY logo on the front. "Well, it seems that you will be the local urchin this summer, so incorporate this goal of yours into delivering these bagels to the bank. Be there in fifteen minutes."

The bag dropped into my arms like a heavy burden. I'd successfully gotten out of a job last summer and I was hoping to do the same this summer. Life is much too short to start work at the tender age of twelve, in my opinion. But by the look on Mama's face, I figured the lot had been cast in my unfortunate direction and would not likely be changed by any amount of dramatic monologues I could conjure up.

But my spirits dragged upon the ground. How was I to find the perfect match for dear Mr. Fisk while burdened with a job? What about Clementine and Miss Wiskerton? It would be near impossible, and I felt very wretched as I entered the bakery to plead my case before Papa, whose romantic nature would surely understand my plight.

"Dearest Papa," I said, finding him in the middle of delivering a chocolate chip croissant to a young man. "Please speak to Mama on my behalf. She's bound to tie me to the world of work this entire summer, while indeed, I need to be about the work of love."

Papa smiled and looked down upon me. "Oh, don't worry, Polly. You'll have fun. And I'm sure you'll find a way to work love, or whatever it is you're talking about."

"Pleeease, Dad," I whined. And though I highly detested to use this tone or these words, my need was desperate.

Papa smiled—"Just a second, Polly girl"—and turned from me to the customer at the counter.

"I've been craving one of your bagel sandwiches," the woman said. "I've fallen madly in love with it and with those chocolate croissants. I just can't get enough."

Fallen madly in love, fallen madly in love, fallen madly in love. The words echoed in my heart, and at once I was revived.

Yes, who could resist a croissant or a similar delectable treat? And what better way to entice young lovers to true and enduring love but with a hand-delivered baked pastry from an admirer? The language of pastries was a language that spanned age and time and senses.

And while delivering delicious baked goods I would keep my eye out for prospective matches for Mr. Fisk, my dearest sister, and Miss Wiskerton.

The revelation was so romantic and full of promise that I was hardly able to contain my joy.

Though moments ago the delivery job seemed like a thorn in my side, it was actually not a burden after all.

It was destiny.

I kissed my father upon his cheek. "Yes, I believe it has much promise, Papa!" And I took up my deliveries and stepped out into the sun that hadn't yet overpowered the breeze with its heat. Then, placing the paper bag in the light brown wicker basket on my bicycle, I set my favorite straw hat with pink roses on top of my head and pushed off down the sidewalk.

I would search this morning for a young woman that would become the missing ingredient in the lives of my bosom friend and her father.

My hopes had faltered a little by the time I arrived at the bank. My back was drenched in tickling perspiration and the only woman I had spied who wasn't already married and chasing after a slew of children s Miss Wiskerton, who seemed to have fallen asleep, for her backside resembled a prize-winning tomato and the seagulls were circling above her.

I pushed through the bank doors and smiled at the cool air that met each drop of moisture on my skin. Though I hated air conditioning with its stale, manufactured air, and much preferred the wild, romantic breeze off the ocean, I had to admit it felt very pleasant at the moment.

I stepped up to the receptionist and smiled. "Here are the bagels you ordered."

The woman, whom I'd seen only a handful of times at the local market, nodded, took the bag of bagels, and spent such time counting and recounting the exact amount of money that I wondered if a job at the bank was really the job for her.

"Here you are. And there's an extra quarter and a lollipop in there for your effort."

"Thank you," I said, and stepped out.

A quarter and a lollipop? I breathed deeply in and out, filled with indignation. Though I was but twelve, I was not so young as to be treated like a child.

I shook my head as I pushed off my bike and headed back home. She had been fair, with a warm smile and straight teeth, but she was permanently off the list of potential women for Fran and her father. The thought of her treating Fran and me like mere children made my blood turn circles and I felt like I could fall into a swoon at any moment.

No, the woman that Fran and her father needed was someone who: was kind, smiled often, knew how to make a variety of recipes, though did *not* like chicken cordon bleu, and treated Fran like a human being and not a child.

Lollipop indeed!

Back at the bakery, Papa was leading my mother in a slow waltz around the empty kitchen, humming in her ear. Mama turned to me as I walked in. "Oh, Polly, you're back already. Here are three other bags of pastries, bagels, and breads to be delivered. I'm glad you found a way of incorporating this into your goal," she said, smiling.

I was beginning to mistrust that smile.

I set the bags in the basket and retreated down the sidewalk on my bicycle once again. All three deliveries were on the boardwalk, which was delightful to all of my senses. So many savory scents intertwined with each other in the air that I was forced to stop for a moment and walk to the end of the small pier. There, with the waves crashing beneath me, the breeze whipping my auburn curls in a swirl around me, and the sun warming my cheeks with a slight rosy tint, I was convinced I was in heaven itself. I imagined a young man with dark hair and stormy eyes touching me on the shoulder.

"My lady? Are you well?" he asked. His eyes were concerned, though a small smile crept upon his lips.

"Why yes, you just startled me," I replied, the light illuminating—

"You okay?" I opened my eyes to find a rather rotund, portly man standing before me, with a beard that was much in need of a trim.

He was not the least like the young man in my daydream, but he did save me from being too terribly late in my deliveries. "Nope, I was just . . . ," I said, walking briskly back to my bike. "Never mind. I'm okay. Thanks . . . I mean, thank you, good sir." And I pedaled off down the weathered wooden boardwalk.

The first two deliveries went well, but I purposefully saved the delivery to Up and Away Kites as my last stop. Mr. Nightquist had owned the shop ever since I could remember, and I adored him more than just about any other person besides my own family and Fran. He had a cheery disposition and reminded me very much of what I envisioned Matthew Cuthbert to be like: generous and kind, round around the middle like a muffin, and sweet as melted chocolate.

When I was little, Mama and I would walk along the boardwalk and stop every afternoon to pay Mr. Nightquist a visit. He had been a family friend before my parents had married, and has known my sister and I ever since we were babes. He had first taught me to fly a kite when I was little and had bequeathed to me his dear wife's leather-bound books (*Pride and Prejudice*, *Jane Eyre*, and *Wuthering Heights*), which were the prizes of my bookshelf.

I'd never known Mrs. Nightquist because she'd died the year before I was born, but he talked of her often, and from the picture he kept by the cash register, I could see she had been a handsome woman with kind eyes and a delicate dimple on her chin.

I grabbed the small paper bag and peered into the shop as I had done since I was able to walk. A loud wail, proceeded by screams and bellows that ruffled my spirit, pierced through the glass window.

The child could be none other than Charles Hildeburg.

Though I despised rolling my eyeballs for any

reason whatsoever, I'm afraid the reaction came naturally and without my permission whenever Charles Hildeburg was a part of the situation.

Dear Mr. Nightquist.

His daughter, Melissa Anne, a young woman I had always had the highest regard for, had locked herself into matrimony with a man who was quite below her in all things. The man called himself Bruiser and his last name, Hildeburg, did not compliment Melissa Anne's name very well at all.

With Bruiser, Melissa Anne had a single child, named Charles, who was widely known in town as having a very disagreeable disposition and the irritating habit of screaming and wailing loudly whenever he did not get what he wanted.

If only I had been able to help Melissa Anne to make a suitable match.

My heart mourned for Mr. Nightquist at the thought of him having to be connected with Charles and Bruiser by blood and by marriage.

The door to the shop blew open, and Charles sprinted onto the boardwalk with a very frazzled Melissa Anne attempting to capture him.

I sighed and smoothed my dress, pinching my cheeks to add just a hint more color to my complexion. Surely the pastry would soothe Mr. Nightquist's soul at least for the time being.

The bell above my head tinkled a greeting as I walked inside.

"Good morning!" a deep voice called from the back. "Welcome to Up and Away Kites!" Mr. Nightquist was cordial to everyone—a quality I prized highly.

"Good morning," I called from the cash register.

"Is that? Could it be?" There was the sound of empty boxes falling to the ground or being kicked out of the way as the voice came closer. "Is it my girl? My Polly girl?"

I felt my cheeks blush a rosy red and I twisted on my heels. Though I hated being treated like a child by everyone else, with Mr. Nightquist I couldn't help but feel six years old again, and honestly I adored it. "Yep, it's me," I said.

He peeked around the side of the wall and smiled. "It is you! My day just took a turn for the better!" I held out the small bag to him, but he took it and flung it on the counter and instead took my hand and twirled me around.

I giggled.

Once he was done twirling me like a top he took the bag and opened it. His eyes closed as he sniffed the bag, the same response that I gave when my mother had finished baking an apple streusel. "Hmmm. There is nothing like a Madassa chocolate croissant and blueberry muffin delivered by my favorite girl in New Jersey to make my day!"

I giggled again, then spied a torn kite atop the counter.

Mr. Nightquist picked it up. "Missy and Charlie came by to visit this morning," he said, holding it up and sighing.

I nodded, "Yes, I saw them depart at quite a speed, though I fear that Charles will win their race, much to Melissa Anne's dismay."

Mr. Nightquist rubbed his balding head and smiled. "Yeah, he's a bit of a challenge."

I bit my tongue quite hard to keep myself from uttering more thoughts on the subject of Charles and his current upbringing.

"And how is your daughter faring?"

He shrugged. "Well, it's always good to see her, even if she thinks I'm an old man that needs looking after."

"Why, whatever do you mean? You are at the height of both fitness and health," I exclaimed.

"Oh, she's got me eating more pills than a horse,

and for some reason she thinks I can't cook a decent meal." He sighed. "She comes over most evenings, which gets a bit much at times. But I know she means well. She just thinks I've been alone too long and I need a mother to take care of me or something." He retrieved the croissant and set it on a napkin. "But enough of that. You'll stay for a bit and keep an old man company?"

I peered down at the small, delicate watch I kept hidden in my dress pocket. "I'm afraid I cannot. Parting is such sweet sorrow," I said, performing an elegant curtsy. "I am afraid that I am tied to the working world this summer."

He waved a hand at me and laughed. "Aren't we all? I'll be sure to order this more often," he said.

"Have a most wonderful day." And I walked out and started for home.

It was only when I passed an older couple holding hands and walking in the sand along the beach that I realized that perhaps Melissa Anne was correct about one thing, though it had nothing to do with having a mother.

Mr. Nightquist, the kindest, dearest, most well-bred older gentleman in all of New Jersey, was utterly, completely, and sadly alone.

Yet my heart leapt with hope inside me. I would find the perfect match for both Mr. Fisk and dear Mr. Nightquist!

And indeed, though I would not hand my beloved Mr. Nightquist to any woman, I could not help but think of the equally lonely Miss Wiskerton.

I smiled.

Love was truly in the air.

chapter six

In Which Love Is in the Making and I Hear a Suspicious Noise

I went straightaway to my bosom friend's home to tell her of my wonderful idea. She would be most excited, I was sure, and I could hardly contain the delicious excitement that bubbled within me.

Once more Mr. Fisk was out in the sunshine, much to my great joy. And indeed, he was hanging an elegant swing on the porch—perfect for two lovers!

My heart nearly burst inside me!

"Well hi, Polly! You looking for Fran?"

I smiled. "Indeed I am, Mr. Fisk. Is she about?"

He laughed quite heartily and pointed to the backyard. "I think she's in the backyard making bracelets."

"Thank you," I said, yet hesitated from moving in that direction a moment longer. "That is quite a lovely swing, I dare say," I said. "Quite cozy and romantic."

Mr. Fisk looked up at me, smiled, and said, "Good, I'm glad you think so," and went back to hanging it up.

I giggled to myself and proceeded to the backyard, where I found my beloved friend swinging in her hammock, a long bracelet made of bright, flowery colors upon her lap. "Oh dear Fran," I declared, rushing to her side. "Would you like to accompany me to Macko's for a delicious Italian meal? I have much to tell you of, and"—at this I could barely contain my excitement, and squealed—"you're going to be so excited, I just know it!"

She swung her legs over the edge and set the bracelet down at once. "Yep, let's go! I'm starving!" And together, hand in hand as bosom friends, we strolled toward the boardwalk.

Fran bit into a piece of Macko's pizza, the cheese stretching out a few inches before breaking apart and hitting her chin with a saucy streak.

"So what do you think is wrong with him?" she asked, though it took me three tries to understand her with her mouth overflowing with pizza.

Her manners were hopeless. Believe me, I have tried to reform her.

I sipped my lemonade, enjoying the clinking of the ice against the glass. "What's wrong with your father?"

"Yeah. I mean, raspberry torte, Polly? Besides the chicken cordon bleu, he's never made anything other than mac and cheese. This is getting serious. So what do you think? Has he told you anything?"

"Indeed, we did converse." I nodded and smiled to myself, then took out the handkerchief and smoothed it with my fingers. "You remember Gilbert and Anne? Or Elizabeth and Darcy? Even Jane and Mr. Bingley?"

She shrugged her shoulders. "Um . . . I think so."

"Well, it is my opinion, and I have kept track of the time since your mother left and of the months your father has been making chicken cordon bleu, that . . ." I paused to mount the tension in the air. "That . . . your father needs to find his Anne. He needs an Elizabeth in his life." The thought sent my heart soaring.

But my dearest Fran was not following me. "Elizabeth who? I don't know any Annes either."

I sighed in exasperation. "I'm speaking figuratively, Fran. What I am trying to say is that your father is ready to love again. And I think it is time for me to find your father a wife and you a mother." I held up my hand to stop her so that I might explain more fully. "And dearest Fran, I know this new woman will never replace the lady who you have called mother from birth and who has cradled you in her arms. This woman will be a confidante, a friend, a loving supporter of all that you are."

"You're kidding, right?" she said, almost laughing. "I wish, Polly, but really, I don't think he's ever going to love someone again. I want him to find someone, I think, but . . . I mean, my mom was . . . she was everything to him." She coughed into her hand and took a quick—and quite loud—sip of her lemonade.

The idea clearly made her nervous. That was understandable.

"Trust me, Fran. I know you might not be able to see it because you are too close to the situation. I, on the other hand, can see the signs clearly. He is desperate to find his true love." My insides melted at the thought.

Though I had never experienced romance for myself, unless you could count the time that Brad Baker kissed me underneath the large oak tree by the kindergarten room several years ago, I'd seen it unfold. And one day I, Polly Madassa, would find my own Gilbert Blythe or Mr. Darcy. But he would not come from around here, I was sure. The only boys in my class civilized enough to carry on a conversation without referring to their buttocks or the sounds that come from those parts were obsessed with a game where they spent ungodly amounts of time in front of the computer naming dragons and attempting to find out where the government has hidden Mount Doom in the land of Mordor or some such nonsense.

I had long since resigned myself to the fact that I would have to rely on the traveling tourists visiting our town or my own destiny to lead me someplace else in order to find a suitable match for myself.

"Polly?"

I jerked my head up. "Sorry, I was just contemplating. Go on."

"Even if he is, which I don't really think so, shouldn't these things just happen like they did in those books?"

I nodded. I had thought of this as well. "Yes, you make a good point. But think: if we did leave the decision up to your father, it would seem that you would have a computer for a mother, because that is the only . . . thing besides you and me that he spends any time with. Really, Fran. Your father doesn't go out anymore ever, and how is he supposed to meet a lady of quality if she doesn't see him and he doesn't see her?"

She wiped her mouth with the napkin and shrugged. "I guess you're right about that. But how are we supposed to find someone for him? It's not like you and I meet a lot of older unmarried women either."

"Another good point. But," I said, with the same flourish I could imagine a great stage actress making, "it just so happens that my mother has given me the task of delivering for the bakery this summer. Every morning till noon I will be bicycling around town, and while I'm out I will be on the lookout for any potential mates." I brushed back a loose auburn curl that fell delicately upon my cheek.

"He won't like it that we're fixing him up, though," Fran said, pouring a pile of ice into her open mouth and crunching down.

"Oh, but we cannot tell him. He mustn't know. This all will be done in secret. Then when they are wed in holy matrimony we will reveal that it was you and I who brought about their union." I sighed and placed my hands on hers (though avoiding the blob of cheese sitting on her index finger). "I, Polly Madassa, do solemnly swear that I will find you the perfect mother and your father the perfect wife. If I do not, I will perish in my shame."

Fran looked at me with eyes that practically begged for my help. She nodded and sighed, betraying the hidden angst I knew brewed below the surface. "All right, Polly. You're the one who's read all those romantic books. But don't get upset if he doesn't fall for the girl. And," she said, pointing her index finger at me, "you need to promise that you'll stop if it doesn't work out."

I smiled. "Of course, though I am sure not to fail you."

That night, alone in my room, I sat at my desk with a sheet of stationery in front of me. The cream-colored paper was bordered with tiny blue flowers and twisted green vines, and I held my favorite calligraphy pen in my hand.

I dipped the pointy silver tip into the small well of black ink and let my pen scratch across the surface. That was my favorite part about the calligraphy pen—the *scritch* sound it made with every letter. I had received the calligraphy set for my birthday and had used it almost every day since. There weren't many things more romantic than a beautiful piece of stationery decorated with the swooping loops and proud marks of words written in calligraphy. Even the word *calligraphy* was romantic. Calligraphy, calligraphy, calligraphy.

I set the sheet down. My dearest friend's happiness, as well as that of Mr. Nightquist, Miss Wiskerton, and Clementine, was of great importance, and I felt hard-pressed to begin at once.

So, at the top of the piece of stationary I wrote:

Project 1.

But that didn't sound quite elegant enough. I put a curvy line through the word and folded the paper neatly in half to be recycled.

After another piece was in front of me, I tapped my chin and found the perfect name for each of the matches I would make that summer:

Love in the Making

I giggled to myself. *L* was probably the most sophisticated-looking letter when written in calligraphy, and on this page, my *L* looked better than the one in the instruction book.

"Mr. Fisk," I said, and wrote his name under the heading. "In need of a wife: able to cook delicious culinary dishes. Clean and neat with a cheery disposition."

Of course, there was no one I knew of who had these qualities and none to whom I would ever hand over my darling Fran to take care of. But my range of knowledge ended with the teachers and various other custodial or refreshment workers at my school. There was Mrs. Miller, Fran's piano teacher, but unfortunately since her recent divorce she was gone for the summer and not likely to return until school commenced. I was convinced there were others, though I could not think of names at the moment.

But I did not let this bring me angst, for I was sure I'd soon find the perfect match for my friend and her father while delivering pastries.

Next, I wrote, "Mr. Nightquist: in need of a wife. Someone able to cook healthy food, with accounting abilities to help with work. Needs to love kites and be able to handle a grandchild who is quite a challenge." Indeed, I hoped Charlie—I mean Charles—would not hinder a match for dear Mr. Nightquist. It would be necessary to conveniently forget to mention Charles to the soon-to-be Mrs. Nightquist until she had given her heart to Mr. Nightquist in its entirety.

Names fluttered in my brain like a butterfly's wings, the main one being Miss Wiskerton. Indeed, she was large and spent most of the summer the color of a pomegranate, but she was kind for the most part, was an excellent cook, and did have a most pleasant smile. Her dog, Jack the Nipper, was the only drawback. Though I knew Mr. Nightquist adored the canine race, Jack the Nipper was an entirely different species unto himself.

Miss Peterson, who taught music at the elementary school, was another likely candidate for Mr. Nightquist. She was pretty and kind, with a sweet, angelic voice. And though I didn't know if she could cook, she had a good taste in pastries, for she often came into the bakery to order the delectable Butter Danish or my favorite: the chocolate éclairs.

I tapped my calligraphy pen against my cheek. This would be harder than I thought. Apart from the kite shop, I rarely saw dear Mr. Nightquist. I was sure, however, that Melissa Anne, Bruiser, and Charles took it upon themselves to visit him most evenings as Mr. Nightquist had said. This would make an attachment to the lovely Miss Wiskerton perhaps a tad complicated. Indeed, Miss Wiskerton rarely left her yard.

But then again, Miss Peterson, the other woman under careful and delicate consideration, lived even farther away—across the harbor—and commuted into our fair town for her employment during the school year.

Yes indeed, the only suitable choice was Miss Wiskerton. She was to be the lucky woman. The image of she and Mr. Nightquist together formed in my mind and I was swept away by the splendid match.

And perhaps I would find a suitable man for Miss Peterson come the start of school.

I circled Miss Wiskerton's name very delicately and added small ivy leaves around the border. Yes, Mr. Nightquist would court Miss Wiskerton.

It was true, there would not be many opportunities for their acquaintance to blossom.

Yet I would not be hindered easily.

I wrote my dear sister's name upon the sheet, but, unable to think of one worthy of her in my acquaintance, I left the space blank.

I blew on the paper and retrieved the special powder that set the ink. But then a noise alerted me to someone in distress outside my door.

It wasn't a loud sound like I often heard when Clementine fixed her hair, and it wasn't the sound of music or the television.

The noise was soft and mournful and seemed to be coming from the bathroom across the hall.

I slipped into my bathrobe, the one with the ruffles around the bottom hem and my initials embroidered on the white satin cloth, and opened my door. I stopped the door at the red tape mark I'd made on the floor last summer when I finally realized that past this point the hinges creaked and I was found out.

Once the door was in place I slipped out into the dark hallway and pressed my ear to the door.

Crying.

Sobbing even, though it was muffled by something—probably a towel.

But from whom?

The toilet flushed, and I dashed back into my room and pulled the door nearly closed with not so much as a moan from the hardwood floor.

My heart thumped in my chest as I watched Clementine retreat to her bedroom. Surely this most recent lament was the result of Clint. Surely there was a suitable gentleman out in the great wide world who would treat her as she deserved? And someone who would not hinder our sisterly friendship.

I stepped into the hallway and toward her door. "Do not fear, Clementine," I whispered. "I will unite you with your one true love."

Indeed, I will bear the task with pride.

Hearing her mourning made me even more assured

that I needed to rid my sister of boring Clint and introduce her to her soul's one true mate.

"Polly, what are you doing?"

As if from a dream, I awoke and found myself gazing toward the ceiling, my delicate hand upon my heart, and Clementine staring at me from her room with a face that I remembered her giving me when I presented her with an embroidered handkerchief for her birthday present.

"Nothing. I was . . ." I composed myself and felt that honest words would be the best thing to say. "I had heard the noise of intense pain and sorrow that can come only from a heart that is not satisfied . . . a heart that is longing for more, a heart that is—"

She rolled her eyes in a manner quite unbecoming. "Polly, what are you talking about? Clint and I just got in a little fight—you wouldn't understand anyway. And I'm fine . . . we're fine, and that's all that matters." At that the door was slammed shut, and I heard her dialing a telephone number from within.

And where was the sister whom I had confided in when I first learned of Mrs. Fisk's attachment to the Internet mother-stealer? I remembered how she took me in her arms and rocked me like a babe. Then she had taken both Fran and me out onto the boardwalk, where we each bought a balloon and partook of vanilla custard. Fran's balloon was now deflated and hung on her wall as a reminder, I am sure, of that whimsical day. I myself had released my balloon into the wild wind, committing Mrs. Fisk forever to a memory.

"And get away from the door, Polly!" Clementine yelled quite loudly, startling me from my memory and bringing me into the painful present of her situation.

And I departed hence to my room, where I thought upon her situation and her obvious misery. She was in desperate need of my assistance in this hour of need.

Love in the making.

Yes, having decided on my course, I would begin my matchmaking on the morrow with earnest.

chapter seven

In Which Fran Gives Me More Distressing News

"You have become a hopeless romantic, just like your father," Mama told me recently when I convinced her to replace my computer with an antique typewriter. "Though I don't think even he would take it this far."

"Computers are a part of life now, Polly," Mr. Lanyard, the computer teacher, had stated at the end of the school year. "You better get used to it." He said this in response to my protestations of being forced to use one. And though I delivered a very well-thought-out monologue on the reasons why I mourned the loss of handwritten letters of communication, and much preferred an elegant library to the wiles of the Internet, leaving him quite speechless, he eventually regained his composure.

"Sit, Miss Madassa," he demanded, to which I promptly sat. But no amount of Googling (such an undignified term) made my opinion of the computer change. I still much preferred the delicious clacking and clicking of the typewriter, or the scratching and scritching of my calligraphy pen.

That is why I highly disapproved of Mr. Fisk's use of time on his laptop and was appalled when Fran gave me some very unfortunate news the following morning.

It was quite early, the sun just kissing the horizon with its first rays, and I was in our kitchen preparing three croissants for two very special young ladies and one special young man, though I was unsure of who exactly one of those young ladies and the young man would be. Still, it was much better to be prepared.

My deliveries would commence in a little over an hour, so I was basking in the joys that baking early in the morning provides for the soul.

I was kneading the dough by hand, much preferring that method to the electric mixer upon the countertop, when I saw Fran's face appear outside the window. She rapped fervently upon the glass, and I came to her at once and opened the door.

"Dearest Fran, whatever is the matter?" Indeed, though my friend was not of a lazy constitution I knew that most days of summer she was not up much before ten o'clock.

"Me and my dad talked until really late last night." She gasped for breath as she said these words, having, most likely, run all the way here. "And I need to tell you something."

"Indeed you do, dearest friend."

"I think . . . I think he found someone."

At these words the dough in my hands grew quite heavy and I almost dropped it to the ground. "What?! But how in the world did he find . . . This is most alarming. But say no more. Indeed, this is not something to discuss here in the kitchen, but rather in the Haven of Heaven." I took the dough back to the counter. "I must finish these croissants and will meet you there in less than half an hour."

Fran departed to Haven of Heaven, a grove of maple trees in the small parklet of town that I had endowed with that name, while I pressed forth with the croissants with an agitated heart.

But how could he have found a young woman already? And how so without aid? Indeed, he rarely left his office or his home. I found the information quite hard to believe and solaced my soul with thoughts that Fran must be mistaken or must have misunderstood her father. Perhaps Mr. Fisk was indeed contemplating a canine companion?

Surely there was an explanation.

Upon placing the croissants aside to rise, I filled a small basket with pastries and a pitcher of homemade orange juice for my meeting with Fran. Then I rushed into the bakery.

"Dearest Clementine," I said. "I must be off at once. There are croissants rising, but I will not be long."

In reply to my plea she merely huffed, and though I think she was forming a haughty reply, I was not able to linger, and left the bakery at once.

Fran sat beneath the Old One, the tree we always met under and which indeed grew tall and appeared quite wise; hence the name.

I set the basket upon the ground, but could contain my questions no longer. "So please, dear Fran, tell me all."

"Well, there isn't too much to say, other than I think he's already found someone," she said.

The green leaves above us acted as a shady shelter and haven against the rising sun. I unloaded the hamper I had provided, and we nibbled and sipped upon the breakfast.

I smoothed my lavender dress and unfolded and refolded my handkerchief in an attempt to remain calm. "And why do you think this, dearest Fran? What were his exact words?"

"Well, last night he came into my room." She took a rather long gulp of the orange juice. "He said he's been chatting with her every day for about a month and that he wanted to get to know her a little better now. He wanted me to know and to see what I thought." She looked at me, her anxiety over the situation showing in the way she twisted and turned the napkin on her lap.

"So this was not about him wanting a dog?"

Fran shook her head. "Definitely not."

But this could not be!

A twinge of sadness twisted my throat. I could not lie and say that I wasn't looking forward to uniting my best friend's father with his forever match. To be a part of the reason two lovers were together was such a romantic thought that I often was lost in the rapturous imaginings.

Then the thought of *how* he had met her struck my mind. As previously mentioned, Mr. Fisk did not often leave his office, nor even his house. "Well, maybe he *has* met someone," I said, proceeding cautiously. After all, she hadn't given me any of the details. "Please, did he say anything else?"

Fran sighed. "I swear, Polly, he had the goofiest smile on his face the entire time. At first I was happy, thinking that maybe he'd really found someone after all. But . . . but then he told me the worst part."

"Worst part? Oh gosh, what is it?" Anxiety was now overtaking me. I composed myself. "Continue, dearest Fran. What is this lady like, if indeed she is a lady?"

"Well, her name is Lovetolaugh."

"Lovetolaugh? What kind of a proper name is that? Surely you meant Miss Lovetolaugh? I can't say it is a much better improvement, but I feel it rather absurd that her father or mother would name their beloved child a noun and a 'to be' verb. Are you quite sure that is her name?"

"Yes. And that's not the worst part. He . . . he met her on the Internet." Tears clung to Fran's delicate lashes.

The phrase came out so fast that it took me a minute to realize just exactly what my very best friend had just said. When the meaning finally hit me, I was stunned into complete silence. The leaves blowing in the gentle ocean breeze barely whispered a rustle, as if they too were in shock.

"Polly?"

"Well . . . Fran . . . this is just not . . ." Words. Where were they?

"I know. I'm really worried. What if . . . what if she takes him away from me, just like my mom?" Tears threatened to spill from her eyes.

Emotions tumbled inside me. "Fran," I said, quiet and soft. I wrapped my arm around her and allowed her head to rest upon my shoulder. As a friend, I would comfort her in her hour of need, but I knew I must be honest with her also. "Fran, this is not good. I remember very well your mother's unfortunate situation. This, my dearest friend, is the . . ." Words failed me. "The . . . exact opposite of love. We must act quickly."

"But—what do I do? I mean, he seems happy—really happy. And I'm—or at least I was—really happy too. It's just been hard not having a—"

I held up my hand. "Say no more, my friend. I know your feelings as if they were my own."

"But you—oh, never mind." Fran sipped on her orange juice then spoke once more. "I'm excited, but on the other hand, I don't know this woman at all. And after my mom left—oh Polly, what should I do?" she asked again, leaning against the trunk of the Old One. Despair was written on her features and the orange juice splashed onto her leg where it was sure to leave a sticky spot on her skin.

"What should you do? Nothing." I handed her a napkin, then embraced her. "I will take care of this unfortunate situation. I will find a woman who will capture your father's heart and soul. This Internet connection will be forever broken when the bonds of true love are formed."

"You think?"

"I am certain, dearest Fran. Now we know that he is indeed ready for love. In that we must rejoice. I will now look for his heart's one true love." I pulled out the small antique watch I kept in the pocket of my dress. Mama would be wondering why I had not started on the deliveries. I slipped my dainty feet inside my white sandals, the ones with the pretty pink rose on the side. I kissed her on the cheek, gathered up the hamper, and placed it in the basket of my bicycle, then climbed on. "Know, Fran, that my eyes are watchful. And do not lose heart, my dearest Fran. It will be all right. This dark day will pass. I shall not fail you!"

Upon arriving at my home, I found a cloud of smoke billowing from under the bakery door and the sound of Clementine's laments from beyond.

I sighed with relief at the knowledge that, because of my deliveries, I would not be forced to mend whatever culinary disaster my sister had conjured up this morning.

Mama whisked into the kitchen, her cheeks a lovely shade of rosebud with an elegant dab of flour upon one side. "You got back just in time, Polly," she said, handing me three bags. "But you better get moving." And then she rushed back into the bakery mumbling something about "charred to a crisp" under her breath.

"Upon my word, Mama," I called after her. "I am off." And after wrapping up one of the croissants with a lovely paper doily, I set off for the elegant Miss Wiskerton.

Said lady was just flipping over to her other side when I leaned my bicycle against her white picket fence and stepped through the gate into her yard. She had exquisite taste in flowers, and I breathed deep the scent of gerbera, lilac, hydrangea, and roses.

"Polly Madassa? Is that you?" She lifted up her

large white sunglasses, then put them back down and readjusted her straw hat on her head. "You know the smoke from your house fills the entire neighborhood? Me and my Jack almost choked to death right in our beds."

Jack the Nipper frantically tugged at the leash that held him fast to Miss Wiskerton's chair. I was thankful for this restraint.

"Please accept my sincerest apologies, Miss Wiskerton. It seems that Clementine was once more baking this morning."

"As I said before, she's going to burn down the house if you're not careful."

I ignored the comment and stepped closer, though still far enough away from Jack that my dainty ankles were protected against his bite. His little lips curled up around his pointed teeth. I hoped Mr. Nightquist and Jack would become fast friends, though Jack was not known to be a kindred spirit with anyone. "I hope you are enjoying your book, Miss Wiskerton?" I asked.

"I am, thank you. And are you starting another Austen novel?"

I sighed. "I plan on reading *Emma* quite soon, but can't seem to stop rereading *Pride and Prejudice.* Truly, each time I read it, it's just as fresh and brimming with romance as the first time I picked it up."

Miss Wiskerton smiled. "Well, I have to say, it's nice talking with someone about novels."

"It is indeed," I said, and then held out the doily-wrapped croissant. "And I am here on additional business as well. I'm here, Miss Wiskerton, on a delivery."

"Delivery?" She sat up and took off her sunglasses. "I didn't order anything from you all."

"Oh, I know you didn't order it, but I'm afraid someone ordered it for you. It was a man and he called early this morning and said specifically to hand-deliver this delicious pastry to one Miss Wiskerton, the Beauty of the Sea."

Her interest was piqued and she smiled. "A man, you say? Are you certain?"

"Indeed, I am quite certain. He phoned just this morning and had me select the most plump and browned croissant in our bakery. I assure you he was most insistent upon the matter. Sounds just like something Mr. Darcy would do, doesn't it?" I asked.

Her cheeks blushed in an elegant manner, and she attempted to hide a shy smile. "Yes, it is. Or Captain Wentworth . . . he's from the book *Persuasion*. Well . . . did he tell you his name?"

I shook my head. "The man did not say. He only

hoped that you would accept this token of his great esteem for you and he would reveal himself if it was accepted with favor." Indeed, though I did not enjoy causing her agitation, I thought it best to add a dash of romantic mystery to this first delivery.

And it seemed to have worked quite well. For Miss Wiskerton accepted the small wrapped pastry from my hands, her fingers trembling with anticipation. She removed the doily and placed a hand on her heart. "Oh, my. It is quite a beautiful-looking croissant, isn't it?" she said.

"If I do say so myself, it is the most perfect one I have ever laid eyes upon."

The lady lifted the pastry to her lips and nibbled the end. "Well, you may tell him thank you and that I accept this token of . . . what was it?"

"His esteem."

"Ah yes," she said. "Thank you very much, Polly."

I performed an elegant curtsy. "You are most welcome, Miss Wiskerton, though I am only the bearer of these romantic tidings. Now, I will leave you to your morning. Good day."

And then I departed her home for the rest of my deliveries, the sweet fragrance of blooming romance pushing me forward.

chapter eight

In Which I Meet Clementine's One True Love

As I rode my bicycle about town, stopping for but a moment at the real estate office, the library, a law firm, and a small bookstore for deliveries, I saw no one worthy of becoming my bosom friend's stepmother, no one to become Mr. Fisk's lifelong companion. This caused me great inward unrest, especially as I remembered my friend's news of just this morning.

In order to save dear Mr. Fisk from the certain ruin that becoming involved with an Internet woman afforded, I needed to find his perfect match...and soon. I sighed and set off for home.

The journey took me past the toy shop, where I was met with a handsome, noble face—one I had not seen before. His dashing smile threw me so off guard that my bicycle swerved, and moments later I found myself lame on the sidewalk.

Footsteps slapping the concrete told me he was coming to my aid, and heat rose in my cheeks. I was not sure whether this was out of embarrassment over my clumsiness or in anticipation of speaking with the young man.

"Here, let me help you," a deep, British-accented voice spoke above me.

I looked up to find his hand reaching for mine, his face obscured by the rays of sun behind his head. I allowed myself to be lifted to my feet and winced at the stinging flesh on my knee.

"Are you all right?"

"Yeah, I guess," I said, brushing off my dress and composing myself. "I am ruffled merely in the flesh. My spirit seems intact."

He laughed, led me into the shop, and pulled out a stool for me to recline upon. "There's a first-aid kit around here somewhere. I'll get you a Band-Aid."

"Oh, I'd hate to impose on you, though the offer is kind."

"No trouble at all. Not every day that a beautiful girl falls down in front of me." He handed me a flower from a vase on the counter. "I'll be right back."

I sighed. His hair was filled with light brown curls, his nose was like that of a prince, and his eyes danced like the aurora borealis. Even his strong cheekbones gave him a distinguished air. His age, however, deterred me from allowing myself to dream much further. Alas, were he but a few years younger, or I a few years older...

But Clementine!

My dearest sister was in need of a gentleman—someone to love and adore her and treat her as a lady. And surely a gentleman such as this who would take care of one younger than he was certain to treat me not as a child like Clint did, but as a young woman.

I held the delicate blossom to my nose and allowed my thoughts to drift into the near future. Dusk settling over the wild ocean. My dearest sister and I, hands locked with each other. This young man strolling beside us, his arm entwined with Clementine's and his heart devoted to her and to all those she held dear.

"Are you okay?"

I came to the present to find the young man's handsome face looking into mine. "Oh yeah, definitely... I was just caught up in the rapturous moment."

He smiled. "Well, I moved here for the summer with my aunt. She owns this store." He walked over to a small sink just like I imagined Mr. Darcy would have done with his dear Elizabeth. He returned, and in one hand he held a goblet of crystal-clear water, in the other a bandage. "So what's your name?"

"Polly. Polly Madassa. And yours?"

"I'm Eddie." He dabbed at my wound with a cleansing salve, then placed the Band-Aid upon my knee before helping me off the stool. "It's very nice to meet you, Polly. I hope we meet again."

Edward, a noble name indeed. I smiled. "Yes. Again, thank you. I would love to return the kindness in some small way."

"Oh no. Don't worry about it. What was I supposed to do for a damsel in distress?"

I slipped off the stool onto a knee that was badly injured though not above repair. "You are very kind, but I must insist you allow me to do a small favor, however small it may be. Please, name your request!"

He laughed, but cradled his noble chin in his hands. "All right. Let me think." He drew closer to me and my heart fluttered. "This is your home, then?"

I nodded.

"Do you know a girl called Tracy Michaels? She works at the bead shop across the street."

I looked up at him. "Yes, she is a friend of my dearest, most beautiful sister. Why do you want to know?"

His defined cheekbones grew red. "Do you know if she's seeing anyone?"

"No, I don't believe so. But again, why do you inquire after her?" I was afraid I knew the answer to my own question, but asked it just the same.

He shrugged his shoulders. "I don't know. She seems . . . nice. I was thinking of asking her out."

No, this would not do at all. This Edward was meant for my Clementine, not for Tracy Michaels, who had a horrible way of contorting her face whenever she was displeased. Besides, she was also known to hold up her fingers in the shape of an *L* and say "loser."

"Asking her out? I am afraid that is most unwise. Tracy is from a very strict family. They . . . they do not allow courting of any kind. Besides, they . . . they still harbor a grudge against England. You know . . . because of the war."

"The Revolutionary War?" he asked.

"Yes, that's the one." I quickly sought to change the subject. "But enough of that. I have thought of an excellent way to repay you. If you could stop by Madassa Bakery on the corner of Seventh Street tomorrow morning, my beautiful sister Clementine will have just pulled out a fresh pan of the most delectable chocolate chip muffins you can imagine."

He shrugged his shoulders. "Hmm. Never heard of anyone still caring about that war," he said. "Oh well. All right, Polly Madassa. I'll be there." He led me outside, grabbing the door for me. Then he held out my bike. "Do you need help home, then?"

This young gentleman was like something from out of a leather-bound book! "I think I can manage."

And with that, I hobbled down the sidewalk, my lips spreading into a wide smile. I could hardly wait to let my dearest Clementine know.

Once at home, I leaned my bicycle against the house and plucked one small posey from among the garden flowers before entering the house. Though roses smelled the most delightful, the word *posey* was one that seemed to melt on my tongue like a very fine dark chocolate.

"Hey Polly, where've you been?" Papa was behind the register, wiping off the counters with a white rag. The bakery had closed just minutes ago, and I feared being enlisted in the unwelcome task of cleaning if I did not make a quick exit.

"Hello, Papa," I said, moving briskly past. "I have been delivering, of course."

"Here, catch!"

I turned around just in time to find a white towel hurtling toward me. It landed, damp with bits of crumbs and stains, on my shoulder. I promptly removed it and held it by my thumb and index finger.

"Wipe down those tables. And don't worry, it won't take long."

I sighed and succumbed to my fate for the next few minutes. "Where's Mama?"

"Oh, I think she's reading. We're going on a date tonight, so you and Clementine are on your own for dinner, okay?" Papa continued cleaning in a manner that was quite vigorous. And I feared that if I imitated him, my own delicate hands would surely blister.

I looked up. "Speaking of my beloved sister, is she here?"

He smiled. "I think she went out with Clint a little bit ago. She'll be back for dinner, though."

I sighed. "That is what I feared."

"What? You don't like Clint?"

"Papa, you jest, I presume? Clint is not suitable for

my sister. He leaves much to be desired, not the least of which is a tenderness toward my sister. She was crying once more last night. And I believe that is the second time this month."

"Oh, Clint's a good guy. And... well, all couples have lovers' spats."

"But not you and Mama. You two are a fairy tale come true."

He looked up and a smile graced his face. A faraway, dreamy look overcame him, and I knew at once he was thinking of Mama... his dearest Judith, his one true love.

"Oh, we had plenty of fights, believe me, especially while we were dating. There was this guy that almost broke us—"

I held up my hand, for I did not wish to hear of my own parents' turmoil in their younger years. "I apologize, dearest Papa, but I do not believe it. You and Mama are indeed a fairy tale."

He smiled. "Well, you are right about that, Polly girl. But why don't you give Clint a chance. Who knows, he might surprise you."

If only he would, was my first thought, but I did not speak it aloud. Instead, I handed Papa the soiled white cloth. "I think I will take a small constitutional, Papa. Is that acceptable?"

"You mean a walk?" He laughed. "Go ahead. Remember, your mom and I will be back later on tonight."

I stepped out into the afternoon sunshine. The wildness of the ocean—the salty breeze, the crashing waves, the rising tide—beckoned me, and I followed its call.

Once I reached the beach, I slipped out of my sandals and let my toes drink in the warm grains of sand. The wild fury of the wilderness excited my heart, and I giggled at the matches I would make for those I loved. I walked to the lapping waves and let my dress drag in the salty ocean water, for nothing is as romantic as a walk on the beach with the surf drenching your ankles and the bottom of your clothing. I lifted my face to the sun, catching the afternoon's rays, and imagined I was on Prince Edward Island, the breeze blowing my natural curls around my face.

"Ah, me," I whispered into the breeze.

"Polly?"

"Huh?!" I whirled around to find Fran before me. Her hair was in a tangled heap around her, and she wore a brand-new multicolored friendship bracelet around her wrist, but still with her cheeks flushed a rosy hue. She was the picture of beauty.

"Polly, what on earth are you doing?"

I lifted my eyes back up to the heavens. "Just drinking in the late-afternoon sun like raindrops on a lily." I locked my arm in hers. "Join me, my dearest friend."

She tugged at my arm, breaking me free from my blissful trance. "Your dad said I'd find you down here."

"Do not worry. I have not neglected my bosom friend and her father. I have been hard at work. Even this"—I gestured to the ocean and my footprints behind me—"is part of the work of love."

She laughed and picked up a shell from the pulling tide. "I'm not worried. I really don't think this will be anything at all. But he did tell me he's going to talk to her on the phone for the first time tonight."

I turned toward her. "And you must listen to their conversation, dearest Fran."

"Really? Why?"

"We must know to what extent your father has attached himself to this woman."

Fran arched her eyebrows. "But Polly, he can't be

that attached to her if this is the first time he's even talked to her on the phone."

I clucked my tongue. "But you must not underestimate the powers of Internet communication, which you are all too familiar with. Indeed, I do find myself worrying about his attachment with this woman." I linked my arm in hers. "Yet despite this unfortunate connection your father has formed, do not lose the dream of having a stepmother and confidante whom you love and who loves you deeply."

"Yeah," she whispered, gazing out into the deep blue ocean. She shrugged her shoulders. "All right. But do you think . . . do you really think that maybe he'll find someone?"

"Indeed, my heart does not doubt it. And though today my efforts were fruitless, tomorrow is another one filled up to the brim with so much possibility."

Fran did not speak more, and after gathering my belongings together we strolled to my house under the cool breeze of dusk.

We stood in front of my home. A small bell tinkled its music on the wind, and I knew supper was about to be served. I'd given my family the dainty crystal bell so that they could call me into the house without shouting like barbarians throughout the neighborhood. Mostly they remembered to comply with my request, and I was pleased Clementine did so now. Shouting would only agitate my peaceful spirit.

"Will you join me and my sister for dinner, Fran? Though it is sure to bear the blackened scars of Clementine's cooking, it will not be the chicken cordon bleu that has become the thorn in your side."

"No thanks, Polly," Fran said. "I better get back. Dad's supposed to talk to the lady tonight, but I don't know when."

"Oh gosh! Yeah, you gotta get home! I mean . . . you must hasten home. Write down everything that is spoken." I squeezed her hands. "And I offer up my thoughts and prayers on your behalf during this hour of trial."

She nodded. "I'll call you tonight."

I entered the kitchen and found my innocent sister Clementine sitting uncomfortably close to Clint. I groaned inwardly. "Hello," I said through clenched teeth, for a lady always keeps her manners, even in the presence of one who does not deserve it. "How good to see you, Clint. You're looking very . . . large today." I swept past and retrieved a kettle of water to boil on the stove for a cup of tea.

He laughed and emptied brown liquid I assumed was some species of cola down his gullet. "And you, my dearest Pol, are as small as a gnat." He was clearly making fun of me, and I was not amused. On the contrary, I seethed.

But I refrained from comment, though the words formed on my tongue and itched to get out.

Clint grabbed a bagel from the basket on the table without even asking if he may. "Well, I'd better go, Clemmy. Call me later and maybe we'll go on a walk to the pier or something."

I straightened, finding a small chance for him to slowly redeem himself in my eyes. "I would love to join you both, if that would be acceptable. It has been much too long since I have been able to spend time with my dearest sister. I promise I will be no trouble."

He looked over at Clementine and laughed, which unfortunately brought an unattractive vein to his forehead. "Is she serious?" he asked. And when Clementine did not answer he reached down and pecked her on the cheek with as much love and passion as if she were a couch cushion and left.

Tears welled in my eyes at the thought of my dearest Clementine chained to a life with a man such as this. She would die of sheer boredom and monotony. And surely I would perish at the loss of my dear sister forever.

"Bye, Clint!" Clementine crooned, and then stood and cleaned up his mess, which consisted of more crumbs and debris than when our baby cousin Chloe pays us a visit.

"I'm surprised you are still involved with that unimaginative nincompoop. Really, Clementine, I am surprised you can endure it. He keeps you from being attached to anyone else, and I am sure you noticed how wretchedly he treated me just then."

"Cut it out, Polly," Clementine said, wiping off the table. "And really, 'nincompoop'? I was hoping you'd be done with the *thee*s and *thou*s by now."

I ignored her rash comment and sat at the table, placing a laced napkin on my lap. "I met a young gentleman who is employed at the toy store today. He's your age, Clementine, and ever so handsome and kind. He adores chocolate chip muffins and, I believe, is planning on calling tomorrow morning. His name is Edward. Imagine, dear Clementine, a prince, and you would not be far from his true image."

"Edward, huh? Well, why is he coming here?"

"Clementine, my darling sister. He is someone who is suited for you. He has manners and an enticing British accent, and he was so kind to aid me in my hour of need."

"Well, why don't you date him then?"

The tea kettle sang out, and I poured a small cup of tea in Mama's roseleaf tea set. I added two lumps of sugar and blew over the top of the tea. "Ah, I would if he was but my age. Unfortunately, years between us will forever be a barrier for any love that we may have had. But really, Clemmy... Clementine, Clint is just like every other boy in the school. He's a bore. Edward? Well, he's perfect for you. And he's coming over tomorrow morn for chocolate chip muffins." I sighed.

She turned to me, a piece of Clint's leftover bagel in her hand. She wagged it at me. "He can come for muffins, but don't you go trying to fix me up with him. Ever since you read that stupid book about prejudice and pride, you've gone completely nuts."

I sipped my tea. "Well, I mourn for you, my dear. And if I am completely nuts for having manners and good taste, then Clementine, I hope to be completely insane." I dabbed at the corners of my mouth. "And I think you will think much differently on the morrow.

Edward is quite a dashing suitor and respectful of me, unlike Clint."

At this she rolled her eyes quite unbecomingly.

She was beyond my help, it seemed. I sighed deeply and smelled . . .

Something burning?

I crinkled up my dainty nose. "Dear Clementine, you perchance have not been . . . cooking something?"

"Oh, crap!" She smacked her hands on the table and dashed for the oven.

She pulled out a blackened shriveled circle and plopped it onto the counter. "Stupid pizza," she said.

I took my leave after wrapping a small red apple from the fruit basket in my lace handkerchief. "Remember about the gentleman who will be calling tomorrow. I do hope you'll do better with the chocolate chip muffins in the morning."

"Oh, shut it, Polly."

chapter nine

In Which I Feel the Weight of My Chosen Task

It was very distressing to continually dial Fran's telephone number and find the line still unavailable. The temptation to bicycle over to her house was almost too much for me to bear, but I resisted. Instead I took refuge in the beauty of words and took up *Pride and Prejudice.* Turning to the delicious scene where Elizabeth finally accepts Mr. Darcy's proposal of marriage, I placed the back of my hand against my forehead and recited aloud the lines from that beloved novel:

Had Elizabeth been able to encounter his eye, she might have seen how well the expression of heartfelt delight, diffused over his face, became him; but, though she could not look, she could listen, and he told her of feelings, which, in proving of what importance she was to him, made his affection every moment more valuable.

I sighed. "Indeed, that is—"

The telephone rang, jolting me from my pleasant contemplation. "Hello, Madassa residence."

"Polly, it's me, Fran."

"Finally!" I sighed in relief. "My dearest Fran. Do you know how I've longed to speak with you these past hours? I'm afraid it put me in such a flurry of emotion that I was forced to recite romantic lines to soothe myself."

"Yeah, sorry. He was on the phone for a while. And well, I listened to most of the conversation, but then I sneezed—you know how my allergies act up in the summer—so Dad told me to get off."

Upon concluding her sentence, she sneezed and I was convinced that this had indeed taken place. "Ah, though I love the buds of spring and the flowers of summer, for this moment I lament their effects on you. Now, what took place this night?"

"Her real name is Ruthie Carmichael and she lives just a few hours away."

"Hmmm. The name suffices, though Ruth is much more distinguished than Ruthie. What else?"

"She laughs a lot, and she works for a dentist."

I shook my head. "*Tsk tsk.* That is not a good sign. I simply cannot imagine your father dating a woman whose hands spend most of the day in other people's mouths. Any other occupation but that one."

"I don't care about the dentist thing so much, it's the fact that I think they are planning on seeing each other . . . and soon."

The adverb hung in the air like a thick cloud of doom. *Soon?* "No way! Are you serious? Um . . . please tell me it isn't so."

"Yeah, I think . . . I think it might even be next weekend."

"You're kidding me! I mean, oh dear! I haven't much time then to introduce your father to his one true love." I placed another beautiful sheet of stationery in front of me in preparation for the work ahead. "But do not fear, dearest friend of my heart. I have already begun to brainstorm. Now it is simply choosing the woman of his dreams."

"Well, maybe you don't have to. She sounded really nice and funny and she even said—"

"Oh no, dearest friend. I know that I must continue. Surely you don't want this woman Ruthie, if indeed that is even her real name, to lead your father astray as your mother was led?"

I was met with silence. Poor Fran, unable to utter a word in such dire circumstances.

"Fran? Are you still there?"

"Yeah. Anyway, Dad wanted me to talk to her on the phone too, sometime this week. I guess so I can get to know her or something."

"I am very sorry for that, Fran. But perhaps I will find a suitable lady of quality for your father before that unfortunate phone call, he will fall in love instantly, and you will be spared the task of conversing with her."

"All right. I better go," Fran said, in a manner that sounded filled with despair and sorrow.

I sought to pluck up her spirits despite this small setback. "I will telephone you tomorrow with the name of that special young woman." I set the receiver down and turned to my calligraphy set.

I pulled out my worn and tattered copy of *Anne of Green Gables*, careful to hold it with the binding down so that pages twenty through eighty would not fall out. Reclining myself upon my satin comforter, I flipped to the middle of the book when Anne first comes to the little schoolhouse and Gilbert lays eyes on her delicate beauty.

The scene graced through my mind like an elegant dance.

He noticed her.

That would need to be my first tactic. They must notice each other. And to accomplish this, the two needed to be in the same place at the same time.

Clementine and Edward would meet in the morn, so I had already accomplished this for my dearest sister and she was sure to be embarking on the wild adventure of love come the next afternoon.

Miss Wiskerton was already filled with love's promise. Tomorrow I would deliver a chocolate Danish for dear Miss Wiskerton and reveal the name of Mr. Nightquist to her.

As for dear Mr. Fisk, I had encountered no woman that met up to his stature. Yet tomorrow, above all else, I would make that my primary task. Time was of the essence.

I heard the kitchen door open below me and quickly stole to my open window. Mama and Papa had returned earlier from their date and had fallen asleep in each other's arms while watching a Cary Grant and Audrey Hepburn movie. Because of this, I knew that it was Clementine and Clint returning from their walk to the pier.

"Good night, Clemmy," Clint said.

I rolled my eyes at his farewell. Did he really have no romantic imagination at all?

"Night, Clint. I love you." He kissed her on her moonlit cheek with the passion and love he'd likely give to his grandmamma (though for Clint to have any such gallantry to the elderly was beyond my realm of imagination).

Clint smiled and said, "I know," and the door closed.

Ugh.

Clementine's footsteps on the stairs brought me away from the window, lest she find me eavesdropping and become even more disagreeable.

There was a soft knock upon my door. "Come in, dear Clementine," I said. And hope sprung anew inside my chest at the thought of her confiding in me—confiding in me that indeed she was not content with Clint and needed my aid... needed my sisterly friendship once more.

The door opened and in she walked, the picture of elegance except for the way her mouth seemed almost to snarl and her bright yellow shirt, which bore the words HOT CHICK on the front. "How did you know it was me?" she asked, placing her hands upon her hips. "Were you eavesdropping again?"

"No indeed, perish the thought."

"Trying on my necklace?"

"Of course not." Though my mind flitted to the beautiful necklace our parents had given Clementine on her sixteenth birthday. I had named it the Amulet of Love because of its great beauty, and though I had wished to try it on, the necklace was not in any of its usual hiding spots.

"Were you looking through my journal then?"

"By all means, no," I said. I hadn't realized she'd taken up writing her daily trials in a diary. I wondered if she kept the Book of her Soul under her mattress cushion as before.

"Polly?"

"Yes, my dear sister?"

"Are you sure you weren't snooping around?"

"Of course not, though I cannot understand why you ask."

"Because I thought I heard someone at the window,

and because you knew it was me at your door, *and* because of the guilty look on your face."

I glanced down and pulled out a fresh sheet of stationery. "I'm sure I don't know what you're talking about. This face is the same face as always."

Clementine laughed just a little, reminding me briefly of how she used to act toward me. "Come on, Polly. Your expression is exactly the same as it was when I found out you'd been reading my journal. The same one that you had on when I caught you taking out all the lightbulbs and hiding them so we'd be forced to use candles."

I allowed a slight smile to grace my face at the memory. "And still I am convinced that any atmosphere is made much more romantic by the flickering light of a candle."

"Well, as long as you're not spying on me, Polly, like you did when I was dating Brent."

Ah, yes. Brent. Clementine and he had many long conversations with one another on the porch just below my window. Indeed, I could have written a book with the information I received from their communications. Brent and I had gotten along quite well, and he often brought back a single pretty chocolate just for me when he and Clementine went out upon the boardwalk.

But unfortunately, Brent had a laugh that could not be endured for any amount of time, and he was much too proud about his family's great riches. I knew the connection could not last.

Clementine moved toward the door. "Good night, Polly."

"Um . . . uh . . . how was your evening walk with Clint?" I asked in an effort to keep my dearest sister in my room just a little longer. In fact it was not so long ago that we shared the same bedroom. Lying awake in the long evenings she and I would giggle and converse or engage in songs until we fell under the moon's hypnotizing gaze. I yearned for those moments to be memories no longer . . . but rather the present.

Clementine stopped at the door and sighed. "It was great."

"Did he offer you flowers?"

"No."

"Offer you a beautiful seashell from the wild surf as a token of his love?"

"No." Her hands went to her hips. "Polly, I know where this is going, so just stop."

"But my dearest, did he give you nothing? Did he say anything that caused your heart to patter within your chest?"

"Of course, Polly."

"What?" I asked, interested in any side of Clint that was not extremely dull.

"Well... I don't know. He said... he said that the moon lit up my hair like a lightbulb." And at that, with no further words on the subject, Clementine departed from my room, slamming my door behind her.

I sat back down upon my bed and took up my pen. Ugh.

A lightbulb?

Her statement only made me more determined to rid my sister of this common boy and introduce her to a gentleman who would sweep her off her feet.

Lightbulb, indeed.

Edward would arrive tomorrow, and if the seed of love did not blossom between them tomorrow morning, I would need to take more drastic measures to save my dearest sister.

Indeed, I needed to save her from herself.

chapter ten

In Which I Deliver a Croissant, Meet the Woman of Mr. Fisk's Dreams, and Fall into a Delightful Swoon at My Accomplishment

I awoke early the next morning to the glorious scents of freshly baked scones, muffins, tarts, and Danishes drifting into my bedroom. Mama or Papa must have arisen before Clementine to take over the baking this summer morn.

"Thank heavens," I sighed, knowing that Edward would be arriving very soon. If he was met with blackened muffins it could not be assumed that he would return to court Clementine.

After slipping into a long light-blue dress and tying the ribbon around my waist, I walked down the stairs. "Mama?"

"She's still asleep, Polly," Clementine called from the kitchen. "Dad's got some deliveries for you to make."

Could it be?

I entered the kitchen to find my sister standing over a silver tray of chocolate chip muffins. I allowed a small smile to grace my face. The power of suggestion, of letting her know that a gentleman was interested in meeting her, had worked.

I walked past her, breathing deep the scent of sugar and chocolate that created an aura around her. "Edward will be most pleased, dearest Clementine."

She sniffed. "Edward? Who's that?"

"Why, the gentleman who will come to call on you this very morning. The one whose muffins those are."

"Um . . . someone is 'calling' on me? Drop it, Polly. These are for Clint." She placed the muffins haphazardly on a tray and plopped them onto the table.

This just would not do.

"But Clemmy! Edward is coming in a few minutes!" I whined, knowing this tone was necessary if she was to be persuaded.

At that moment, the door in the bakery tinkled. "That is surely him, for a gentleman is never late. Dearest Clementine, you must meet him, just this once," I said, placing in her hand a small vial of lip gloss called Antique Pink. "You must. He is most anxious to meet you. And my dear, it will do no harm."

I breezed through the kitchen door and found that indeed it was Edward. His eyes gazed into the glass case filled with pastries and he turned to me, offering a dashing smile.

I blushed. "Why Edward, it is so good of you to come."

"Yeah, um . . . thanks, Polly. I have to get to work in a few minutes, so I'll take—"

"Oh, I do understand. And fortunate for you, my beautiful sister Clementine has just pulled a most delectable tray of chocolate chip muffins from the oven. If you will just wait here in the foyer, I will ask for her assistance."

He shrugged his shoulders.

"Come on, Clementine!" I whispered, pulling her by the sleeve in a most indelicate manner toward the door. I took up the serving tray from Mama's tea set (the edges lined with a delicate trim of olive-green ivy) and arranged four of the plumpest and most delicious-looking muffins on top. I placed this in Clementine's hand and shoved her through the door.

I followed after her but was stopped by a hand on my shoulder.

"Morning, Polly! Did you see the deliveries for today?"

I peeked my head through the door and saw the two in a locked gaze of love. I smiled and answered Papa's inquiry, "Yes, Papa. If you will give me but a minute. I am in the midst of love in the making and mustn't disturb its tender bud."

Papa laughed and pulled me from the door, much to my dismay.

"But Dad!"

"I know, I know." He placed the brown sacks in my hands. "But you have to get going. I will watch over—what did you call it?—the tender bud of love?"

I sighed and accepted my burden, though inwardly I was longing to see Clementine and Edward locked in true love's embrace.

"Now go ahead before we start getting calls about where the food is."

Indeed he was right. Their voices were much too low for me to be able to decipher what was being said. "Yes, I have other tasks to attend to," I whispered. "Two other romances to see to."

I set the delivery bag on the counter. Selecting the most attractive chocolate Danish, I placed it on a square piece of wax paper, folded the edges up neatly, and then fastened the bundle with a satin bow I had brought down from my dressing table.

Clementine was on the brink of a romantic relationship with the dashing Edward, and I was assured of an even more successful morning and afternoon.

Love was indeed thick in the air. And I would do my utmost to harness its power for Mr. Fisk and Mr. Nightquist.

Miss Wiskerton was once more upon her lawn chair, though I noticed her hair done in a very elegant style with a small lily tucked into her curls.

"Good morning, Miss Wiskerton. I hope you are well?"

She sat up straighter and smiled. "Hi, Polly. I'm . . . I'm good. And what are you doing riding around this early?" Though she tried to hide it, I witnessed her cheeks blush to a pinkish hue, which quite became her complexion. Jane Austen's book *Persuasion* sat upon her lap, and her dainty hand rested upon the cover.

"Why, I am delivering pastries this morning. And once more I have heard from your admirer and am here to deliver a most delicious Danish to the object of his affection."

"Oh, indeed?" she said.

"Yes, that is what he said. The gentleman owns the

kite shop on the boardwalk, I believe. He sounded very pleasant and kind. Just as Mr. Darcy himself might sound if he were a little bit older, and born in America, and owned a kite shop."

"That would be Peter Nightquist." She tapped a pink nail against her chin. "Hmmm. He and I never got along in high school. He married Miriam, and she was such a wonderful woman. You know, I did see him at the grocery store a month back and he said I looked very... healthy."

I nodded. "You must be correct. And though I know nothing of any unfortunate past you may have with the gentleman, he did insist on having this pastry delivered to you." I held out the pastry, proud of my handiwork and presentation. Indeed, it was quite beautiful.

She took the pastry and the corners of her mouth rose with a smile. "Ooh, I do love a good Danish now and then. You can tell him I said thank you."

I started back to my bicycle, hardly able to contain the excitement that poured out of me. "Oh, dear Miss Wiskerton, you will have to thank him yourself. For I fear my day is completely occupied with these delectable deliveries. But Mr. Nightquist is employed all day long at the kite shop, and I have the utmost confidence that he would be delighted to see your face and give you a tour of his most wondrous shop."

"We'll see," she said, nibbling on the corner of the Danish. "Thank you, Polly. And make sure that sister of yours stays away from the oven. I don't want to die in my bed some morning asphyxiated by toxic sugar fumes."

"Yes, ma'am," I called out to her, and then pedaled down the street.

I drank in deeply the warm salty air, letting it fill my lungs. The day was shaping up beautifully.

I had found my true life's calling—to bring lovers together.

And though I knew much of my time would be devoted entirely to the task, it was a burden I was proud to bear.

"Hey, it's Clemmy's sister. How are you?" Clint's voice from behind nearly knocked me off my bicycle, and I narrowly missed an oncoming elderly woman in a motorized wheelchair.

I came to an abrupt halt, dismounted, then smoothed out my rumpled dress before turning to face Clint. "Was your intent to knock me off my bicycle and render me unconscious or to merely have me put the life of a distinguished elderly woman at risk?" I curled my upper lip to show my distaste for him.

He shrugged his bulky shoulders, reminding me of an oversized ox. "I just saw you coming down the street and thought—"

I lifted my delicate nose into the air, marking him with my distain. "Really, Clint, as if you and I have much to say to each other. I am like dear Elizabeth, and you, sir, have the romanticism of Mr. Collins, who I assure you was not well—"

He then very rudely interrupted my dialogue and laughed. "Mr. Collins? That's not even my name. You're too funny, Pol."

Pol? Ugh, the name was as hideous said as it was spelled. Brad Baker had attempted to call me that in kindergarten and that had been the end of our brief romance.

I lifted my nose in the air and turned to go. "It would be well for you to know that my sister's affections for you are waning. A handsome gentleman called upon her this very morning, and she was quite taken with his dashing looks and his gentle manner. Now, good day."

His meaty hands reached out to stop me, but I

dodged his attempt. "Huh? You're not serious, are you?"

I grabbed the handles of my bicycle and started down the sidewalk. "I most certainly am serious. Therefore, I think it wise for you to stop pursuing my sister further. She is done with you."

"Come on, Polly. You're kidding, right?"

I turned to look at him. And though my heart wrenched at the look of sadness that had fallen on his face, I remembered quickly the number of times that my dearest sister was burdened with hot tears. "Again, I say that I am not kidding. Now if you will excuse me, I must get going."

Clint's face had turned a shade of scarlet I had seen only as a lipstick in my mother's boudoir. "If that guy thinks he can take away my girl, he's got another thing coming." And he stalked down the sidewalk—a scorned lover.

Oh, to be Clementine—that two gentlemen (or one, since I do not put Clint in that category) would duel for my love.

I continued on my way, imagining the scene in my head.

Two gentlemen, swords in hand, fighting for my honor and the love of my heart.

"I will fight to the death for her hand," one would say. And the slashing of swords would commence. And when the slain suitor lay fallen on the ground I would run to him, and with his last breath he would look into my eyes and declare once more his love. Then I would give him my handkerchief, which he would clutch to his breast, and he would breathe no more.

I could hardly think of anything more romantic.

So engrossed in my imaginings was I that I passed the bank, which was to be my first delivery, and the real estate office, which was to be my second. Once I realized my mistake, I returned promptly to the bank and completed the delivery. But as I started for the door, I was met with the most elegant woman I had ever seen in my small ocean town.

She was tall, and thin, though not so thin as to appear frail and undernourished. A wide straw hat sat on a head that was covered in soft blonde curls that fell gently to her shoulders. Her dress was long, and fair, and on her feet were dainty white sandals. She smiled widely at me and nodded, as only a cultured woman would do. But what was better still was the accent with which she spoke. She could have been a descendant of Jane Austen herself.

"Hello, love," she said softly to the receptionist. "Has Fredrick come in to work yet?"

The woman shook her head. "Nope, not yet, Lucy... I mean, Miss Penny. But I'll let you know when he does."

Lucy Penny?! Why, this was she, the one true love that would capture Mr. Fisk's heart with one glance! I smiled and lingered by the receptionist, pretending to fiddle with my satin bow.

"Well, I'm off to run some errands, so could you just tell him I'll be at the Corner Deli at twelve? Thanks!" And she whisked past me and out into the ocean breeze.

Lucy Penny, to be at the Corner Deli at twelve! Fate was on my side. I glanced at the small watch in my pocket and continued with my deliveries. I had but three hours to decide a course of action for dear Mr. Fisk.

Upon finishing the deliveries, I retired to Fran's house in a flurry of excitement and anticipation. After leaning my bicycle against the elegant picket fence bordering her house, I hastily found my bosom friend and we retired to the backyard.

"I have found her, Fran," I said, grasping her hands in mine.

We reclined on the hammock, the ocean breeze rocking us gently back and forth.

"Really? Who is she?"

"Her name"—I paused for dramatic effect—"her name is Lucy Penny. Is there a more elegant and lovely name than Lucy Penny?"

Fran shrugged her shoulders. "It's pretty nice. Ruthie is nice, too, don't you think?"

I crinkled my nose. "It suffices, though it's not nearly as elegant as Lucy."

"So, what does she look like?"

"Close your eyes," I said, and I did as well, leaning my head back against the swing. "Imagine, Fran. You and your beloved father standing next to an Englishwoman. Her hair is golden as the sun's rays, curls cascading down her shoulders in tiny ringlets, a hat of straw upon her dainty head. A wide smile spreading across a face as beautiful and noble as that of a goddess. Your father embraces her and they kiss, then envelope you, their darling daughter, and myself, your bosom friend. Can you imagine anything so perfect?"

She giggled. "Oh Polly, you're so dramatic. But you're right. It does sound good. Honestly, I wasn't sure you'd find someone, but maybe you did." She twirled a loosened thread from her torn jean shorts. "Is she really that great?"

"Great is not a word to describe her. She is more so, my dear. More so!" I checked my watch again and stood. "And in but one hour, I will meet her and begin sowing the seed of love in her heart. By nightfall, her heart will be at the gracious mercy of your father."

"Can I come along?"

I hesitated, reaching down and plucking a pansy from the small bed of flowers. But I did not speak. Was it wise to bring Fran along?

"Come on, Polly. I mean, if she's going to be my stepmother I think I should at least get to see her. This is a big deal for me. You already have a mother, and I haven't had one for three whole years."

"Say no more." I lifted my hand out for her to join me. "See her you shall, Fran. But you must promise to allow me to do my work."

We started down the sidewalk. "All right."

I sighed and locked my arm through hers. "Today, dear Fran, is a most glorious day for you and your new motherly confidante."

chapter eleven

In Which I Am Pursued by a Secret Admirer and My Beloved Friend Is Secured an Adoring Stepmother

Fran and I made our way to the front of her house, passing by a small bed of lilies of the valley. The delicate white bells hung like drops of dew from the elegant green stalk, and I knew at once what I would do upon meeting Miss Penny in just a little under one hour.

"Oh, they are darling," I said, plucking a handful of the flowers and bringing them to my nose. "If I know Miss Penny, and I am sure I do, we being like-minded, she will adore this gesture from your father."

"But Polly, my dad didn't really give her—"

I placed a hand to her mouth. "*Tsk*, my dear Fran. Remember, you have vowed that you will not hinder the gift I seek to bequeath upon you and your father."

She shrugged her shoulders, and I scanned the beds of flowers. From the garden I chose a single delicate red rose to offset the purity of the white, as well as the small tiny flower that resembled frost on the ground from afar. Then removing the white ribbon from my own hair and wrapping it around the bouquet, I held the display out for Fran to gaze upon.

"It's pretty. But use this instead." She held out a new bracelet she had completed.

Indeed, though the bracelet was made with elegant pink thread, the ribbon was much more becoming. Yet I allowed her this gesture and smiled.

"Very beautiful indeed, dear Fran." I breathed in the scent of the bouquet. "But now we must make haste to the delicatessen or we may miss her entirely."

"Can I ride your bike? Mine's still not fixed from when my dad ran over it with the car."

"But of course, Fran. I weep over your misfortune, for it is such a refreshing feeling to have the wind kiss your face and the blood rush through your veins from exertion."

"Oh, come on, Polly. It's not that bad. Ooh, what's this?" Fran pulled a wilted pink rose from the inside of my bike basket. Attached to the flower with black string was a stark blue piece of paper. "'For Polly

Madassa, the love of my life,'" Fran read aloud. "Polly, do you have a boyfriend you never told me about?"

"Certainly not! I know nothing of a suitor except at this moment." I took the rose, my heart rising at the thought of such romance, and opened the paper.

The paper is blue

And the rose is pink

"He knows how to state the obvious," I said. I coughed into my hand and continued, though the words did not improve.

I love you forever

Like a flower that stinks.

Fran let out quite an unattractive guffaw at the conclusion of the poorly written poem, if that indeed was what it was. "You do! You have an admirer!"

I folded the small paper and placed both it and the flower back in the basket of my bicycle. "This," I said, pointing to the paper, "this, you think, would excite me? Indeed, quite the contrary. I have been insulted to the utmost degree. If he is an admirer, he would be better off showing his affections to someone other than myself. The prince who shall come for me would never declare his love with a wilting rose and a poem with the word *stink* in it. Now come along, Fran. We must be about the business of real romance." And with that, I started down the sidewalk, the heels of my sandals clicking on the cement in rhythm with the beating of my heart.

It was indeed a wonderful thing to be pursued, though it was unfortunate my admirer was not a true gentleman, something that was first on a long list of traits I wished of a suitor. He was, however, very secretive and mysterious, things that were also very high on my list. I crushed the desire to know this young man. His words clearly spoke that though he had affection for me, I would not be the damsel to fall in love with him. No, I must stay on my task, and this one with Fran was of much importance.

"Polly? Polly!"

My thoughts returned to the sidewalk and I found Fran behind me, pointing at a building.

"Huh?"

"Isn't this the deli?"

"Pardon?" I looked up and saw at once that indeed we were in front of the very deli where Miss Penny would be dining. With one glance at my watch, I saw that we had arrived none too soon.

"Why, yes it is, Fran. My apologies for passing by.

My brain seems in a tremulous activity of thoughts."

"Tremulous thoughts of *him*," she said, raising her eyebrows up and down.

"Perish the thought, Fran. And please, never again bring up the letter or the vainly hopeful suitor who has written it." I took her by the hand and strolled into the small dining area filled with the scents of tomato and lettuce, grilled chicken and humus. My own stomach growled at the delightful scents, for in my haste of the morning I had forgotten the nourishment of my own body.

But now was not the time. Romance was my sustenance and love my drink.

Within the small restaurant, dear Miss Lucy Penny sat straight upon her chair, delicate glasses gracing her small, perfect nose, with a hardbound book—possibly leather—before her on the table. If my suspicions of her elegance and supreme upbringing were correct, she was reading the elegant Jane Austen.

A true kindred spirit, I was sure.

"There she is, Fran," I whispered into her ear. "Your soon-to-be mother. Isn't she lovely?"

"Her? The one with the mouth that looks like a frog?"

I gasped, the image bringing up a dreadful remembrance of being chased by an amphibian in the hands of one Brad Baker. "Oh dear me, no, and please, Fran, you know how sensitive I am to such talk. The dazzlingly beautiful woman in the pink dress."

"Oh, her? Yeah, she is pretty."

"And so much more, I am sure." I turned my bosom friend toward me, lifting the bouquet between us. "Now, my dear Fran. It is time for me to speak with her. I ache for your prayers on my behalf that I might not fail you, though my heart indeed feels eager to burst inside my chest with rapturous happiness."

"Don't worry, you'll be fine. You always are. But are you sure that . . . you know . . . this is okay?"

"But of course. Love has no boundaries, Fran. Once your father knows of this, he will be eternally grateful to us. Love is in the air, and I am its vessel." I squeezed her hand once and set off for the table where the lovely Miss Lucy Penny sat.

My mind whirled with romantic visions. She would smell the flowers. Mr. Fisk's name would ring in the air like church bells. Her cheeks would blush to a rosy pink. Their first date. Their magical wedding day. Fran and myself adorned with light-yellow dresses, releasing wild butterflies into the crisp blue air.

It would be a fairy tale come true.

"Hey, Polly!"

The voice startled me. I was reluctant to turn and see who had interrupted my reverie.

Brad Baker. He looked shorter than when last I saw him, though his nose was still rather hooked and his feathery hair gave him the appearance of a bird of prey. I nodded. "Oh hi, Brad . . . Bradley. I hope you are doing well this summer."

He smiled, almost blinding me with the unsightly metallic braces on his teeth. Though time had darkened his eyes to a handsome ocean blue, I could not say the braces added much to the attractiveness of his appearance. "I'm doing all right," he said, stuffing three Cheetos into his mouth. "I'm gonna visit my dad and his girlfriend in a few weeks, but otherwise I'm here if you ever . . ."

I peered over at Miss Penny with all earnestness. Really, I hadn't much time to engage in conversation. "Well, I am sure you will have a wonderful time on your travels."

"Yeah." He gazed down at his cheese-covered fingers. "Well, how's your summer going?"

"Pleasant as expected, though not without its trials and tribulations."

"Huh? Oh, yeah. I forgot you like talking like those people in old books."

I cringed. His manners and upbringing had not improved since school let out. "It was... nice to see you, but now, I really must be going."

"Well, um... do you maybe... would you... um, yeah, hope I see you around."

I nodded and set off once again to Lucy Penny, attempting to herd my thoughts away from cheese-filled braces and back to the luscious pastures of romance.

I strode over to the lovely Miss Penny and offered my bouquet of fragrant posies.

"Pardon me, I do not mean to interrupt your meditations on this beautiful day, but a gentleman, the father of that beautiful motherless girl, asked me to deliver this to you, Miss... Miss..."

"Miss Penny, but... you can call me Lucy." She smiled at me and gestured graciously toward the seat across from her own, as I thought she might.

This I politely refused. "Oh, thank you, Miss Penny, you are much too kind, but really I must be going. My task was merely to deliver these flowers to you."

She brought the bouquet to her face, and I was

pleased to see that I had chosen the flowers well. "Yes, they are beautiful. Lily of the valley is my favorite. Who did you say sent them?"

"A Mr. George Fisk. Isn't that a handsome name? He is a very distinguished gentleman who has the highest regard for you. And his daughter handmade that beautiful bracelet just for you."

"Oh, it's lovely." She looked around the deli. "Is Mr. Fisk here?"

"No, Miss, unfortunately he is not. Being of a shy nature, he wanted your first encounter with him to be based solely on his admiration for your beauty and demeanor. In my opinion, it would be so mysterious and romantic to have an admirer like him. But do not fear, he has assured me that if you receive his gesture with favor, he will make further arrangements to meet you."

She smiled. "Well, that is very mysterious and . . . I have to say, romantic too." She giggled. "You can tell him that—how did you say it? His gesture was met with favor."

I allowed myself a small smile, though I tried to contain my elation within propriety. "I will tell him, Miss Penny. And his happiness will be beyond words. Good day."

"You too," she called after me.

I dashed up to my dear Fran, narrowly missing a great bear of a man who stalked through the deli.

"My dearest Fran! She accepts your father's gift with favor and is anxious to make his acquaintance."

Fran's lips spread into a wide smile. "Wow, really?"

"But of course. So, what say you to this situation?"

She locked her arm in mine and we strolled from the deli to the cobbled street. "Well, I think . . . I think it's great, Polly. I can't wait to meet her. But what do you think we should tell my dad?"

"Do not fear, I have thought on this as well, though I must ponder but a little longer. Be assured, however, that by the end of the week, you, my beloved friend, will have secured for yourself a most wonderful step-mother."

chapter twelve

In Which Mr. Nightquist Is Burdened by an Unappetizing Tuna Fish Casserole

The sun beat down upon our shoulders as we strolled along the sidewalk. Delicious happiness seeped from my skin like lavender perfume over such a wonderful meeting with Miss Lucy Penny. Love was indeed invigorating to the spirit, mind, and body. Right then, I sought to further refresh myself and my dearest friend. "Fran, wouldn't you adore an afternoon at the beach together? Shall we go and bask in the success of your father's future wife, and relish how lovely she is?"

Fran smiled and nodded. "All right! That does sound good. It's getting hotter by the minute."

After changing into our swimming attire (my bathing suit a delicate pink and trimmed with ruffles), we retired to the sand beside the jetty, the spot I now called the Faithful Stone Pathway, for it was far from the clustered crowds and close to the spraying water that hit the jagged rocks with much determination and flourish.

I laid my pure white towel with the pink freesia flowers lining the ruffled border on the sand and began applying my sunblock. Fran, however, in her eagerness to refresh her perspiring forehead, dropped her towel and dashed into the surf.

"Come on, Polly! It feels great!" she declared, her arms splashing pell-mell in the white-crested waves.

"Yes, in time, my dearest friend. However, one can never be too careful with one's skin." And I continued applying sunblock upon my young, untainted arms. Though Fran had a nice brown pigment to her own complexion, I did not seek to grow into womanhood looking as raisiny as dear Miss Wiskerton.

I set my sunglasses on the end of my nose and placed my straw hat upon my head. The tails of the bow hung down my back like an elegant waterfall, and I walked into the surf. The cool water lapped at my toes and I felt enraptured at the tiny sand clams that reburied themselves after each wave exposed them.

Fran joined me at the water's edge. "So how's Clementine?"

"Oh, I meant to explain it all to you last night. My dear sister is also in desperate need of my assistance."

"Really?"

"Oh yes. Her situation is most urgent," I replied.

"But I thought she was dating Clint. They've been together for a while, and haven't they been in love since, like, second grade?"

"Unfortunately, what you say is true. But I have determined that Clint is not suitable for my sister." I gazed out to the sea, letting the breeze blow my curly locks behind me. "He is boring and mundane. When I'm done, my dear sister will be clasping hands with a young gentleman named Edward, whom I met just the other day on one of my deliveries. He aided me when I had an unfortunate tumble off my bicycle." I giggled. "He's so cute . . . I mean dashing. He has an English accent and is a gentleman in every sense of the word. He is perfect for Clementine, and I know he will not treat me with scorn as Clint has done."

"Oh, Clint's just joking around with you, Polly. And besides, does Clementine even like the guy you met?"

I sighed. "If not by now, she will. I am sure of this."

"But Polly, you're not going to break her and Clint up, are you?"

I felt my face flush underneath the brim of my sunbonnet. "Indeed no . . . not necessarily. But their relationship is on the verge of disintegration anyway. I shall . . . shall merely help it along."

"I don't believe it. Clementine would never dump Clint, and Clint would be an idiot if he ever dumped her. I'm sorry, Polly. But I don't think it's going to work. And besides, you should just leave them alone."

"Oh, they'll be fine. I adore my sister and only yearn for her very best. But enough of this talk. Just know that it will result in something out of a fairy tale."

"You better watch out, Polly. If Clemmy finds out, she's going to kill you."

"But do not worry for me, dear Fran. I am convinced of the opposite. Clementine will instead be ever grateful to me and perhaps even name her and Edward's first daughter Polly."

At that, we both reclined upon the sand, letting the gentle sun kiss our skin, and stayed talking with one another until most of the tourists had retired to their beach houses.

"I better go," Fran said, flapping her towel to shake

out the sand. "I'm supposed to talk to that Ruthie woman tonight."

"But surely this is not the phone call where you are to speak with her?"

"Yep," she said. "I was supposed to talk to her tomorrow, but she can't, I guess."

"Oh, my dearest Fran. If only I had met Lucy Penny just hours earlier I might have saved you the grief of talking to this Internet vixen."

"It's fine, Polly. I don't mind that much. If she's anything like what my dad says, she's really great."

"Well, I will offer up prayers on your behalf. Be strong and courageous, my dearest friend. And call me when you are done." We walked to the boardwalk and I kissed her on her cheek. "Until tomorrow, my bosom friend."

I started for my cottage when my eyes fell upon a very handsome young man carrying a kite down the stairs and onto the beach. Tearing my eyes away from his dark, wind-tousled hair, I remembered dear Mr. Nightquist. If I hurried to his quaint shop I would be able to converse with him for a few minutes.

The time felt right for me to introduce the idea of dear Miss Wiskerton and pique Mr. Nightquist's own interest.

"Well, if it isn't my own Polly. How are you?" He rubbed his chin and smiled, then looked back down at the kite he had been tinkering with.

"I am very well, indeed. I just spent an afternoon at the beach with my dearest friend, enjoying the singing of the waves upon my spirit and the kisses of the wind upon my soul. Has all fared well at the kite shop?"

"Yep. It's been good. Slow in the morning, busy in the afternoon, and then it'll start back up in a few hours."

"Have you had any... unexpected guests?" I tried not to look into his eyes and instead inspected a small metal keychain by the register.

"No one that stood out besides Charlie and Missy." He held up a paper plate covered in clear saran wrapping. "She brought me some leftovers for lunch."

"But by the appearance of the dish, you have not touched a morsel!" I declared, worried that perhaps Mr. Nightquist was unwell.

He laughed. "Don't worry, I'm fine. It's just after you've had tuna casserole for the fourth time in one week, it gets a little old. You know what I mean?"

I clucked my tongue. "Indeed I do. And I find tuna to be a most unpleasant fish, especially when the meat is removed from a small tin can that resembles cat food."

He laughed again. "My thoughts exactly."

I sighed. "So no other esteemed guests have stopped by this afternoon besides your daughter baring the fishy lunch casserole?"

Mr. Nightquist looked up and tapped his fingers on the wooden countertop. "Well, come to think of it. That woman, oh, what's her name? Miss Wiskerton. She came in and said she was fascinated by kites and that she loved croissants."

"You don't say? I know her well, and I have come to find that she is quite an exceptional woman of propriety as well as excellent in the culinary arts. Quite a kindred spirit, I assure you."

"Mmm-hmm." Were those his cheeks blushing rosy red at the thought of her?

Indeed, it was evident from the way his fingers fumbled with the delicate fabric of the kite that his feelings for Miss Wiskerton had surprised even him.

I continued. "She lives very near to my own home and has a canine named Jack. He's very... tolerable." I could not immediately reveal that Jack was not of the most affectionate nature. "I also believe that Miss Wiskerton has never married, which I find hard to grasp, since she is of such a wonderful disposition."

"Is that so? You know, I went to school with that woman. She was nosy and harsh when we were young. That's why I hardly recognized her when she came in with a smile on her face. But when my wife was alive she liked her all right. That was enough for me. I remember she came to the funeral, but since then I haven't seen much of her."

"Is that so?" I sighed. "I often wish that I had known your dearest wife, for she sounds wonderful."

He took up a small, framed picture of her that he kept by the cash register. "She was wonderful all right."

"And you miss her still?" My spirits temporarily deflated. I had not thought of this possibility—the fact that Mr. Nightquist might not be ready yet for an attachment.

"Oh, I'll always miss her. I know that. But life goes on, and she wouldn't want me thinking and being sad all the time."

I nodded. "Indeed, I think not. In fact, I'm sure she would want you to be happy in life and in love."

He seemed to smile. "Maybe. Yeah, Miss Wiskerton seemed real interested in kites."

I beamed. How proud I was of dear Miss Wiskerton. "You know, she mentioned the desire to experience the thrill of flying a kite just this morning when I called upon her. Perhaps you would be the person to teach her."

He gazed up at me over the rim of his glasses and smiled, then looked back down. "You mean a date?"

"No, not necessarily. Just a mere meeting wherein the two of you can converse, get to know each other, fly beautiful kites. Then perhaps—"

"Fall in love, huh?" He laughed. "I don't know. I've been out of that game for a long time. Getting back in now is a little daunting."

The longing for love filled the air like the wind beneath a kite, and I grasped at its tendrils. "I can only imagine. But you are so dear, and the very greatest of men. What woman would not want to be on your arm, and the object of your esteemed affection? And from your own lips you told me that your dear late wife wanted your happiness after she was gone from this earth."

He blushed. "And it seems like you've been reading her books, haven't you?"

I nodded. "Her taste in books was exquisite."

"Well, I can't say that I understand everything you've been saying, but it suits you."

"I am glad you approve." I glanced at my watch in

my pocket and realized it was time to depart. I walked behind the counter and kissed him on his balding forehead. "I must go now. But I will see you soon. And please consider the possibility of Miss Wiskerton. I attest to her character."

He nodded and smiled his lopsided grin. "All right, Polly. See you soon."

Back in the open sea air, I breathed deeply and fully, my heart throbbing over the romance blossoming in the kite shop.

Miss Wiskerton and Mr. Nightquist betrothed to one another. The scene was a vision in front of me. White flowers cascading around the twisted branches of an arch. Miss Wiskerton barefoot upon the sand, her long white dress trailing behind her. Mr. Nightquist awaiting her at the end of an aisle lined with rocks and shells from the depth of the ocean's heart. And there I was, walking in front of his future wife, tossing pure white flowers into the breeze, an ivory dress adorning my frame, a pale pink ribbon around my waist, a garland of wildflowers festooning my wind-tousled auburn curls. And wearing Clementine's Amulet of Love around my neck.

I sighed and pedaled toward home, letting love propel me from behind like a summer's kiss.

chapter thirteen

In Which Dearest Clementine Is Filled with Sorrow, I Am Threatened, and I Take Matters into My Own Delicate Hands

Upon entering the threshold of my home I was met with intense wailing and moaning. Mama and Papa sat side by side at the table, hands clasped and conversing in whispered tones.

My heart jumped inside my chest. "What's wrong?" I asked, rushing to their sides. "Did something happen?"

Mama smiled. "Clementine and Clint are in another fight, that's all. They'll be all right, I'm sure. Clementine's just . . . emotional right now."

I sighed, thankful that it was nothing of greater concern. It was probably due to the fact that Clementine broke up with Clint to be with Edward and was now feeling sorry for Clint's broken heart. "Is this because of Edward?" I asked.

Mama's eyes crinkled. "Edward? Who's he?"

"Why, the gentleman who called on Clementine just this morning. I was sure of their match from the start."

"No, it has nothing to do with that. At least not that I know of," Mama said.

Papa shrugged his shoulders. "That boy came and went. He did say he loved the muffins, though. What were you trying to do, Polly, get them together?"

"Well, perhaps. But he is quite a nice gentleman and so much more suited for Clementine than Clint is."

Papa turned toward me. "Just let them be, Polly. If they're supposed to break up, they will. If not, there's nothing you or anyone else can do to stop it."

"Very well," I said, pushing his words from my thoughts. Indeed I would not let my sister chain herself to a man that would forever burden and bore her heart. Yes, I would be the one to stop it.

And the sorrowful fact that Clementine did not entertain Edward as I had instructed her to was more of my concern at the moment. I felt my face flush red. "So what in the world is Clementine wailing about up there?"

"They got in a fight, that's all I know."

Treating Edward, a gentleman suitor, in such a fashion! He must think she was ever so rude. I twirled on my heels to the door. "Excuse me, Mama and Papa. I need to speak with my sister."

The crying had desisted slightly by the time I reached her bedroom, but I heard her voice urgent on the telephone. "She what? My sister? Oh she did, did she? Well, don't believe a word of it, Clint!"

I knew at once that Clint had spoken to my dearest sister about our conversation, and I readily made haste to my bedroom and locked myself inside for refuge.

Within seconds, Clementine's pounding fist thundered on my door. "Polly, you better come out here now! I can't believe you told Clint about that kid that came into the shop! I'm going to kill you."

"But dearest Clementine! It was only you I was thinking of!" I pleaded through the door.

She paid me no heed. "Polly! Come out here!"

But I stayed still, unwilling to let her wrath inside.

"Well, you better tell Clint the truth. That you made it all up. You hear me?"

"But Clementine, I cannot. He is not your heart's true love. I know this!"

"Call him, Polly!" I could almost hear the fire of her anger in every word.

"All right, all right." Yet still, I did not open the

door. "I'll call him tomorrow. Who knows, maybe by then you'll realize I'm right."

"Don't push it, Polly. I'm gonna kill you if I hear you doing or saying anything else."

"But Clementine, please do not be so hasty," I yelled through the door. "Maybe you and I could go and converse about all of this at the Haven of Heaven like we used to do. Remember? We used to be the best of sisterly friends."

But her ears didn't hear me, for her heavy footsteps had retreated into her room and she'd slammed her door with a hollow slap.

I sighed, clutching my pounding heart. Life had almost ended for me, I was sure. But could I do it? Could I call Clint and tell him I had made a grave mistake?

I walked to my bed and took up the box of stationery upon which I had written my plans for Clementine.

Edward and Clementine. Truly, their names together were like music. Could I be willing to sacrifice Clementine's happiness for all eternity for a moment of happiness at this moment? I thought of his comment on her hair shining like a lightbulb.

No, I could not.

In that light, it made everything even more clear to me.

I must intercede on her behalf, and to do that, greater action must be taken. I pulled out a sheet of stationery and took up my pen.

Dear Clint, I wrote. *I am sorry to wound you so deeply. But I must sever all ties. . . .*

But no, that would not do. Clementine would never speak in such a fashion (more's the pity). I folded up the sheet neatly and set it down. Instead I took out a sheet of notebook paper and a very unromantic ball-point pen.

Hey Clint, I wrote. *Sorry, but I'm dumping you. I hope you're not too mad. Have a good life. Clemmy*

Yes, that would do. But I would need to write a note also to Clementine from Clint. This letter, I knew, would break her heart for a short while. But really it was for her greater good. Years from now, with her own little girl (likely named Polly) sitting on her knee, she would utter thanks to me for this.

I sighed and wrote the same note over again except with "Dear Clementine" at the beginning and "Clint" at the end.

I hoped my attempt at a sloppily written note

would convince Clementine that it was from him and not me, her adoring sister.

I gazed upon my handiwork. Indeed, it was not pleasant, but had to be done. "For love," I declared aloud. The gentle wind ruffled my curtains and kissed my cheek. Surely, it was a blessing upon what I had determined to do.

The telephone rang and I jumped at the sound. Indeed, it might be Fran! "Hello, the Madassa residence."

"Polly, it's me, Fran."

"Oh, my dearest friend! I can hear the despair in your voice. Tell me, what new tragedy has struck on this midsummer's eve?"

"Well, he just got off the phone with Ruthie and is waltzing around the living room. Polly, he seems to adore her."

"That is what I feared. We will just have to move forward with my plan and hope that it isn't too late. With a woman as distinguished as Miss Lucy Penny, I do not lose hope. Is there any other information you can give me? Did you speak with this Ruthie as you thought?"

"Yep. And she . . . she's actually really nice. She

laughs a lot, but not too much. And she sent me a letter with a picture of her in it. She put it in a bottle, which was really cool. I got it this afternoon. And tonight we talked about all kinds of things, and she was so easy to talk to. I kinda—"

"Is this so?" I did not expect this outcome in the least. Not only was this a great surprise, but very discouraging. Fran and her father were likely becoming hoodwinked by the computer woman, and disaster was the only outcome I foresaw. "I fear, Fran, that though she laughs and has sent you a message in a bottle, this does not make her worthy to be your mother and your father's wife. I will remind you once more of your mother and the Internet man she met."

There was a slight pause on the other line. "Yeah, I remember. But I don't think—"

"Please, do tell me what else you have found out about this woman."

"Well, she's allergic to cats. She loves the beach and the mountains. She knits and makes quilts and loves old movies. She's also taking an acting class."

"And what is her appearance?" I was confident that even though her interests were to be admired she could not be more elegant than Miss Penny. Still, I feared that Mr. Fisk might be taken by mere outward beauty.

"Well, she's pretty normal looking. She has long black hair and bright green eyes. Her smile is nice."

"Hmm, the description of her is of a highly suspicious nature. How about her teeth?"

"The top ones are pretty straight, but the bottom ones are a little crooked. They're really white, though."

The temptation to bicycle over immediately was almost too overwhelming. Curiosity often plagued my soul more than I could bear.

"So, do you approve of this woman? Because I must say that I think it much too early in knowing anything about her to make a proper decision. I, for one, am highly suspicious of the whole matter. Yet do you approve, dearest Fran?"

"I . . . I don't know. I think I do . . . but really I still don't know her very well. And I haven't met her or anything. Maybe if I talk to her again, I'll know for sure."

"Well, then I will continue to plan a meeting between Lucy Penny and your father. I am still confident that my choice will prove far superior to any woman your father has found on the computer."

"All right, Polly. I guess it couldn't hurt." She yawned very loudly into the phone. "I better go. Call me tomorrow, okay?"

"Yes, of course. Farewell, dear Fran."

I laid my head upon my pillow, allowing my curls to splay out across the ivory sheets. I needed much rest. For tomorrow was a new day, and with this new development with Mr. Fisk and the woman Ruthie Carmichael, I needed to have my whole being alert to the task of uniting Lucy Penny to Mr. Fisk.

My bosom friend's future rested in my hands.

chapter fourteen

In Which My Day Continues to Get Better Moment by Moment

Upon the morn, I felt refreshed and rested, all at once very alive and brimming over with adoration of love's simple and romantic ways. Light as a feather, I skipped down the stairwell and met Mama with a kiss on her rose-petal cheek.

"Thanks, Polly. Now here are today's deliveries," she said, setting the brown bag on the countertop.

"But of course, Mama."

I held the letter for Clementine in my hand and placed it by the front door. Surely she would find it this very day and I would make sure to comfort her when next I saw her.

And though to think of my sister weeping saddened my heart, I was hopeful and delighted at the prospect of her meeting her one true love, Edward. And I was sure that by the evening, the sisterly bond between us would be mended.

Papa came into the kitchen at that moment, bearing in his hands another magnificent batch of chocolate chip muffins. He spun Mama around the kitchen and then kissed me on the cheek. At the prospect of what was to happen this day, all the love that would be kindled, I was at once overcome with joy. I grasped both Papa's and Mama's hands in my own.

"Dear Papa, you are angelically good, and my lovely Mama, you are divinely beautiful. I thank the stars and sun and moon, the waves that crash upon the shore, the geese that fly through the heavens, the—"

"All right, Polly. What's this about?" My monologue was abruptly interrupted by Mama. "I've already said no to buying you a horse and carriage. It's simply not going to happen."

"No, I am not inquiring about the carriage, though maybe we can discuss that at another date. I was merely thanking life in its various forms for the love that is working even now. But, of course, you do not know all that has happened. And when you do, I want not a word of praise. For it is my duty and my burden, which I bear proudly for those I love."

At that, Papa departed the kitchen with a smile. Mama squeezed my hands and sighed. "I'm not sure exactly what you just said, but . . . all right?"

I kissed her dimpled cheek and watched her fill the coffeepot with fresh grounds.

These pleasant thoughts brought me back once more to the unfortunate letter of admiration from the previous afternoon.

I wondered if my own admirer realized his efforts were in vain, or if he would continue his pursuit.

Only time would tell.

I lingered over the brown bag Mama had handed me, my cheeks blushing at the thought of being wooed, even if it was by an unwanted admirer.

I held the paper bag and twirled around, allowing my dress to swirl out around me like a delicate cloud.

"Polly? What in the world are you doing?" Mama stood in the doorway.

"Just basking in another day filled with joy, and laughter, and love."

"Well, please bask your way to these deliveries before I make you pay for them yourself."

"I am at your service, Mama." And with that, I

selected two of our most delicious pastries: an orange cranberry croissant and a Danish filled with smooth, honeyed butter the color of a toasted almond.

Miss Wiskerton and Miss Penny would be receiving another token of love from the men who adored them. I knew that upon this day Miss Wiskerton and Mr. Nightquist would meet, as well as Mr. Fisk and Miss Penny.

And now with dear Clementine, Mr. Fisk, and Mr. Nightquist on the verge of everlasting bliss, I was upon the cusp of joy so profound that—

"Polly?! You're still here? What is taking you so long?" Mama said, startling me to attention.

And with not a word, I departed the house toward Miss Wiskerton's yard.

The genteel woman was outside, as was her usual habit, though I was relieved to find that she was not sizzling on the sun chair. Rather, she sat upon the porch swing fiddling with something in her lap while Jack the Nipper sat by her plump little ankles.

"Good morning, Miss Wiskerton. How are you and young Jack faring this wonderful summer day?"

"Oh, just fine. I finished *Persuasion* this morning and just started *Pride and Prejudice* again."

"Miss Wiskerton, that is most wonderful! We must

talk often as you read through it." I stepped closer so that I was able to see what it was she was occupied with.

Was that a kite she held in her hand? Upon my word, it was! Oh, my dearest lady was indeed in love.

I placed my bicycle upon the ground and stepped through the gate, receiving a rather unwelcome growl from Jack, who, thankfully, was properly restrained. I held out the small package identical to the one from yesterday. "I hope you have not eaten yet, for Mr. Nightquist had hoped that this gift would be a nourishment for not only your body but also your soul."

She looked up and set the kite to one side of her, then lifted herself out of the swing. Her softly wrinkled cheeks had a rosy hue to them that was quite becoming to her face. If dear Miss Wiskerton could just be rid of her current clothing and rather adorn herself in a flowing dress that would tousle with the wind, Mr. Nightquist would be quite pleased, I was sure.

"Oh, isn't he the sweetest, dearest thing?"

I nodded. "Yes, he is." I walked back down the walkway and lifted my bicycle from the earth. "I only fear for his body's health at times."

"Why's that?"

I sighed, and shook my head. "His dear daughter,

Melissa Anne, though with the best of intentions, provides Mr. Nightquist with meals. Unfortunately, she, like Clementine, was not endowed with the gift of cooking or baking. For days, he has had nothing nourishing besides tuna casserole, which, as you may guess, is a dish that can be tolerated but once a year."

"Oh, poor man."

"Indeed. But yet, I have heard of your own skill in the culinary arts! Perhaps you can concoct some savory dish that will awaken his taste buds!"

Miss Wiskerton's cheeks blushed red. "Oh, I don't know that I'm that good . . . but I do know how to make something other than tuna casserole."

"Then you must bring it to him this very evening!" I declared.

"Well, I don't know. If he isn't expecting anything then—"

"Oh, but I am remiss for not telling you sooner! He actually instructed me to tell you that he would be most delighted if you would rendezvous with him this very evening—that he would count it the one joy of his heart." Surely this would not be a difficult arrangement to make.

"Like a date?"

I nodded with enthusiasm. "But of course."

She fidgeted with the box in her hand. "Oh, I don't know. I haven't gone on a . . . date in a long, long time. This is all so . . . so new."

I leaned my bicycle back down to the ground, walked over, and grasped her large hands in my own dainty ones. "Do not fret, my dearest Miss Wiskerton. He is filled with adoration for you. Let love guide you this evening, and may it find you and he locked in a forever embrace."

And with that I left her so that she might continue to dream.

After leaving the genteel woman's home, I went straightaway to Clint's house and, finding the porch empty and windows still darkened, placed the note on the mat in front of the door.

I felt little guilt over my actions, knowing that what I did, I did for my dear sister's best.

Hence, I completed the other deliveries and was fortunate indeed to find Miss Lucy Penny at the bank once again, that being her place of employment.

Dear Miss Lucy was speaking with the great bulging man I had seen just yesterday at the delicatessen. Though my ears strained to hear their conversation, I was thwarted in my attempt by the man's bulk, which was like a great barrier between me and the future Mrs. Lucy Fisk.

When he departed, dear Miss Penny seemed quite despondent in spirits. But I approached her just the same, sure that the croissant and the invitation from Mr. Fisk would serve to delight her and lift up any of her heart's troubles.

"Miss Lucy Penny?" I said as I approached her. "It is I, Miss Polly Madassa, here to deliver this token of affection from the gentleman, Mr. Fisk."

Her downcast face lit up at once with hope. "Oh, really? That's very nice. The flowers from yesterday look beautiful on my desk." She gestured to a dark wood desk, her name written on a small sign, and the beautiful flowers in a colorful array in a small crystal vase. And she even wore the small bracelet around her dainty wrist!

"Mr. Fisk will be delighted to know that his gift has brought joy to your heart. And now this he gives you." I handed her the small box, which she unwrapped.

"This looks delicious. I've heard Madassa Bakery is one of the best in town. Please tell him I said thank you."

"But you may tell him yourself, dear Miss Penny. For

he requests your presence at his home upon the morrow for a cordial visit of tea and other pastries catered by the aforementioned bakery, at four o'clock. Here is his address. He asks that I get your answer that he may make the proper arrangements fitting for such an elegant woman."

Miss Lucy's cheeks blushed. "I must confess that this is odd. I actually already have a . . . at least I think, though I'm not quite sure . . . but . . . but why not?" She stood up tall and lifted her perfect nose into the air. "You can tell Mr. Fisk that I accept."

I smiled. "Really? Awesome! I mean, you have made his heart soar to the highest of heights. I will tell him at once. Good day."

And I left her, turning but once to find her daydreaming out the window into the sunshine and taking ladylike nibbles from the pastry.

Once in the outdoors, I squealed with rapturous delight upon the prospect of their meeting.

"Hey, Polly!"

At once I was brought to reality to find Brad Baker standing beside my bicycle, a dozen wilting dandelions in his soiled hands.

Surely this could not be!

But alas, it was.

He shoved the weeds at me with little ceremony. "Here, Polly. I picked these for you. They were the biggest ones on the sidewalk."

I picked the flowers from his hand with my thumb and forefinger. "Why, thank you, Bradley. That is... very kind of you." Surely he was the admirer of just yesterday!

He laughed a metallic laugh and then held my bicycle out to me. "I know. Hey, you mind if I call you sometime? Maybe tonight, and we can talk about... about the olden times or something. My dad used to have an Afro when he was in college, you know. And my grandpa, he's even older than that."

"Indeed?" I placed the flowers inside my woven basket. My heart trembled within my breast. The unpleasant task of letting down the young lad had me much perturbed and unsettled in spirit.

"I... I am afraid I cannot commit to any telephone calls about your family genealogy at this time. Please enjoy yourself, and perhaps I may see you when school, once again, commences in the fall. Good day." And with great grace I mounted my bicycle and pedaled down the road at a tremendous speed.

When I reached the boardwalk, I stepped down

from my bicycle and fastened it to a post. Though the thought of Brad Baker as my beau was one I detested, I could not help but feel considerably saddened of heart by the obvious devastation he must now feel.

I imagined him pulling out my school portrait from within the pocket of his shirt, holding it close to his heart, and allowing but a few tears to fall down his ruddy cheeks over his unrequited love. Later, as the dark night settled over his cottage, he would sneak out of his room and place my picture within a glass bottle alongside a note that declared:

None other will I love, but this fair maiden.

And tossing it into the retreating waves, he would call into the harsh wind, "Great sea, take my love, and my heart, into thy depths!"

Oh, I did hope that afterward, he would not toss himself into the crashing waves, though the idea sounded wildly romantic.

But I was not able to continue my thoughts, for a young boy dashed past me, nearly knocking me to the ground. The force of his insolent blow sent my straw hat flying off my head and into the sand.

"Oh, Polly girl! I'm so sorry!" It was Mr. Nightquist rushing toward me. "Did he hurt you?"

"No, thankfully he did not." I brushed off my dress and attempted to compose my figure. "Who was that undisciplined boy?"

Melissa Anne dashed up to us, her hair in a wild nest of knots atop her head. She handed Mr. Nightquist a dish. "Here, hold this—it's for you anyway. Now, where did he go, Dad?"

Oh, dear! It must have been Charles who attempted to assassinate me. I had insulted my dearest friend's grandson!

Mr. Nightquist smiled at me and pointed in the last direction we had seen the boy run.

"See you later, Dad. Bye, Polly!" And off Melissa Anne darted, calling out, "Charlie! Be good for Mommy and come back! Come on, Boo-Boo Bear! I'll buy you an ice cream."

My faced flushed red at my poor behavior. "I'm sorry, Mr. Nightquist. I didn't know it was Charlie . . . I mean Charles."

He waved his hand in the air. "No worries. He's a handful, but he's also my grandson and I love 'im, so what can you do?"

"And you are the very best of grandfathers, I am sure. But again, I'm sorry—"

"No more, Polly!" he said, and picked up my hat and handed it to me. "So, where were you headed before Charlie almost knocked you over?"

"Actually, dear sir, I was on my way to call on you, my oldest and dearest of friends."

"Well, what do you know? I'm on my way to the shop if you'd like to come along." And he held out his arm to me, which I took, and we walked side by side into the afternoon breeze. "Why was I the lucky gent you were coming to see today?"

"Because you are the dearest and sweetest." I ceased and lifted my head to the sky in search of words. "And I bring you tidings from Miss Wiskerton, that fair, elegant lady who abides close to my own home."

"Oh, really?"

I snuck a small glance at his face and saw it fill with excitement. Surely, his eyes were twinkling at the very thought of her!

"Why yes. Speaking to her this morning, I have found that she longs with every fiber of her being to learn the art of letting loose a kite into the wild wind."

"Is that so? I never would've thought her the type."

"But nevertheless I speak truth. She is to be at Pier Three this very evening in hopes that you will rendezvous with her and reveal to her your secrets."

"Hmm. Tonight, eh?"

"Yes, Mr. Nightquist. This very night." The images of this evening's meeting excited my spirits, and I forgot about the fact that I almost died at the hand of a six-year-old. "And she plans on cooking you something that will make your taste buds soar to the heights of the clouds. Please say that you will meet her."

"Well, let's see. My shop closes around eight or so. And I'm not sure if I can stomach Melissa Anne's tuna casserole." He held up the dish she had given him.

"But surely you can save the dish for another evening. And I know you can close just a moment or two early to meet with the fair lady. Her heart is nearly driven mad in its frustrated love."

"Wow, I guess when you put it that way. I don't want any frustrated love on my hands, and it'll be nice to eat something different." He turned to me and nodded. "I'll be there at seven thirty."

In my elation over the intended meeting, I pulled Mr. Nightquist's round head down and kissed him on the forehead. Then I spun around, my dress again billowing out around me. "Oh, you have made a young woman's day. I must tell her at once! Adieu, Mr. Nightquist. Adieu!"

And with that I fluttered back to my bicycle, with love as my wings.

I relayed the news of the evening's events to Miss Wiskerton, who was quite pleased, as I knew she would be.

"I already have chicken Marsala cooking in the oven. Do you think that's a good dish?"

My own mouth watered at the sound of the delicious chicken-and-mushroom concoction. "Dear Miss Wiskerton, it is beyond perfection. The chicken is a very elegant fowl, and much preferable to its ocean counterpart: tuna, the chicken of the sea."

"Um...very good. Now what should I wear?" she asked, her full cheeks blushing in anticipation.

"I would suggest an elegant, antique-pink dress," I said. "Though I am convinced that Mr. Nightquist will be enchanted by your beauty in whatever you decide."

She offered a pleasant smile and disappeared inside her house.

My own home was silent upon my return, except for the quiet sobbing of my dear sister in her bedroom.

My spirit ached at her distress, but I composed myself. Her disappointment was something I had expected. "Yet this is for her greater good," I whispered to my own heart.

After smoothing my dress and rehearsing an initial air of shock, I knocked gently on her door and entered. Clementine lay upon her stomach, her eyes lined with red and fresh tears spilling upon her cheeks. A rather unsightly display of soiled tissues surrounded her.

"Dearest Clementine, whatever is wrong?" My heart wrenched in my chest. Indeed, it was I who had brought about such intense sorrow.

Had I done right?

I shook my head. My course had been set, and I must stay upon it. If I revealed what I had done at this moment, I was sure to not make it out of the house with my heart still beating. No, I was sure. Clint was not for my Clementine. Edward was the love of her heart.

She sniffled and blew her dainty nose on what appeared to be her bedsheet, then fell into a despairing sob that shook her shoulders and cut me to the quick.

I sat beside her, careful not to sit upon the tissues, and stroked her tangled mess of hair. "What's wrong?"

"Oh, it's Clint. He broke up with me! Can you believe it? And after you told him that the thing with that Edward kid wasn't really true."

I paused in remembrance of that expectation and was relieved when she did not question me about whether I had actually performed that task.

"I know that this is heartbreaking for you indeed. But know that I am here for you during this hour of grief, and Edward, that gentleman, has passed along these sentiments as well."

"But how does he know about me and Clint?" Clementine asked.

"Um . . . well, he does not know, of course, but I'm sure he *would* say that if he knew. Indeed, he states that he will wait till the end of the world for you. And indeed, I know he speaks the truth only from his heart."

"Just leave me alone, Polly."

But I yearned to linger a little longer beside my sister's bed of mourning. "Maybe," I said, "you and I could order some pizza and eat it by the ocean. We could go shopping for ribbons, then collect shells or something, just like we used to do." I was getting quite taken away by my own plans. "Perhaps, dear Clementine, that would soothe your tortured soul?"

She looked up at me, a clear stream of mucus pouring out of one nostril in a highly disgusting manner. "Well," she said. "Maybe. At least it'll take my mind off of Clint. But I can't tomorrow just in case he calls, and the next night Tracy and I are going out. And if Clint calls, I'll cancel anything!"

And at the mention of his name, she once more fell in a wailing heap upon her pillow.

I stood, quite pleased that at least she and I would be close sisters once more. "I will leave you now, dear sister. Two evenings hence, I will make sure that you have such a pleasant time that you will forget Clint's name forever."

And I departed.

Outside my good sister's door, I smiled and realized that two nights from now was the perfect time to ask if dear, handsome Edward would join us.

The vision was clear in my mind: The three of us laughing by the ocean waves. My sister confiding in me of her love for Edward. Edward confiding in me of his feelings for Clementine. Their hands reaching for the same perfect seashell. Eyes locked, love ignited.

"Ahh," I sighed aloud.

I would have allowed my thoughts to linger on these shores if I had not been in desperate need of speaking with Edward. His well-bred sentiments would surely lift Clementine's spirits and ease her heart's pain. And I hoped he would accept the invitation.

I found the gentleman at the toy store, employed in restocking puzzles of all sorts.

"Hey there, Polly!" he said in the dashing British accent that made my heart melt inside of me. "Good to see you! You know, I loved those muffins the other day. Two thumbs up from me."

I nodded and smiled. "I'm glad you did. But Edward, my heart is crushed inside me!"

"Really?" he asked, still stocking the shelves. "Why's that?"

He did not think me serious, I was sure. "It is my dearest sister. I'm sure you saw her the other morning, the girl whose beauty is beyond compare."

"Yeah, I think I did. She was really nice. What's wrong with her?"

I sighed. "I am not sure. Her heart is broken. She has been treated quite harshly by a boy, and well . . . I think she is in need of tender words of care." He did not speak, so I continued. "I know I have not known you long, but I assure you that Clementine has the highest opinion of you. It would mean the world to her if you, an English gentleman, would give her a few words of comfort that would soothe her troubled soul."

"Me? Huh. Well, I guess so, if it'll make her feel better. I don't want to give her the wrong opinion of things, though, if you know what I mean."

"Indeed I do. And I assure you she would not." I said these words, knowing full well that both Edward and Clementine would fall madly in love, despite the fact that neither one, at this moment, was interested. "If you would come by tomorrow morning, I will make sure that freshly baked muffins are waiting upon your arrival. Indeed, it will mean so much to her."

He smiled and lifted up an armful of puzzles. "All right. I'll be there."

"Oh, that's great... I mean, that is most wonderful." I turned to the door and remembered the outing Clementine and I planned on making in a few days. "Dear Edward, I was also wondering if you would like to accompany my dear sister and me two evenings from now. As young children we often ordered pizza and ate it by the wild open sea. Then we collected seashells together and made necklaces out of them. I am sure this will help heal her wounded heart. We would so love the company of such a gentleman as yourself."

He set the puzzles down and scratched at his most perfect head of hair. "Hmm. I'm not sure if I can do that since I work then. But I'll see if I can get off if you want. Maybe . . . maybe her best friend, Tracy, could come along?"

I shook my head fervently. "I am afraid that would be impossible, Edward. I believe she is . . . is already attached to another young man at the moment."

He shrugged his shoulders. "Oh, well. It would be fun to get out for a bit. I'll see what I can do about work, okay?"

"I look forward to it." And though I held out my hand that he may kiss it, he misunderstood and shook it quite vigorously instead. "Good day, Edward, and thank you with all my heart."

And at that I departed for Fran's home. Indeed, I could not help but skip with joy at love's promising future.

chapter fifteen

In Which I Find Myself Held Captive by a Tree, and Horrible, Unromantic Clint Interferes Once More

Could a day be more beautiful? More filled with the fruits of hard labor and goodwill? I could imagine no such day as I pulled into my bosom friend's driveway and imagined the next afternoon when Mr. Fisk would meet dear Miss Lucy Penny.

"Thank you, Polly," Mr. Fisk would say, lifting me upon his shoulders. Miss Penny would kiss my cheek and say, "It's all because of you, dear, that I, at last, found love. How can we ever thank you?"

"But I need no thanks, for it was all a burden I was—"

"Polly?"

I awoke from my daydream and found I had sat myself down in the middle of a patch of the most gorgeous of gerberas, their bright faces encouraging my heart.

"Polly, why are you sitting in the flowers?" Fran looked down at me from her post at her window.

"It seems I have wandered into a dream, dear Fran! May I come up?"

"Course, you know you don't have to ask!"

I looked at the large maple, standing proud like a gentleman at a ball, and thought how delicious and terrifying it would be to climb its rough bark. And so instead of taking the stairs, I embarked on the romantic adventure of climbing up to Fran's room. It was something I imagined Anne Shirley would do on Prince Edward Island.

But upon climbing the first five feet, I found that the task was quite a bit more terrifying than delicious. The ground beneath me seemed to spread into a chasm, and Fran's bedroom window became a pinnacle that could not be reached.

"Fran!" I shouted. "Help me! I mean... I am in need of your assistance, if you please!"

"Polly? Where are you?"

I heard Fran's faint call of distress over what had happened to her bosom friend and was forced to shout louder than decency allowed. "*Fran!* I am held captive in this large tree. If you could please assist me with a ladder, I would be very appreciative."

As a ladder was brought I was met with the voice of Bradley Baker from below. "Polly, is that you?"

Attempting to remain dignified while perched in the tree, I grasped tighter to the limb. "Yes, it is I."

"Well, do you need me to help . . . I mean, rescue you?"

"Rescue me? Indeed, the idea is a romantic one, though completely unnecessary."

At that moment Fran came to my aid with her father behind her. They made quick conversation as my hands splintered and my dainty muscles cried out for relief.

"Please," I called out. "If someone would assist me, I would be most grateful."

"Oh, sorry Polly," Fran called up. "We'll get you down in a second."

"I'll see you later, Polly," Bradley said. "Maybe next time it'll be my turn to rescue you." And off he sauntered.

"Ooo, rescue you, huh?" Fran called up to me.

"Please do not, Fran. He hoped only to assist me, I believe," I said as I was placed on solid ground with the help of Mr. Fisk's protective arms. "Thank you," I said.

"So he likes you, huh?" Fran lifted both eyebrows up and down.

"If so, I am afraid he will be sorely disappointed." I straightened my dress with trembling hands. "Now if you please, I would like to sit down somewhere."

"So, why were you climbing up the tree?" It was dear Mr. Fisk, who graciously handed me a cool cup of lemonade to refresh me.

"The tree is much too glorious, and I was filled with such overwhelming temptation that I began to climb its knobby bark. But the branch whereon I sat is much higher than it appears from below. Though I cannot say that temptation will not get the better of me again, I will not dare attempt climbing a tree for a long while."

Mr. Fisk laughed. "Just be careful." He then bustled into his office and promptly shut the door.

Fran and I retired to her room.

I sat upon a small stool, rested my head in my hands, and looked out through the window, much like I imagined Anne looking out over Green Gables. "Oh Fran. What a day filled with love. I have been quite busy, you know."

"Really? Did you see Lucy again today?"

My excitement could not be restrained, and I ran to clasp her hands as she sat on the bed. "Indeed I have. And that very same lady accepts your father's invitation to afternoon tea on the morrow!"

"Really?" Her face was distorted with complexity. Though her mouth was turned up in the elegant smile that I had come to adore, she turned her eyes to the bedspread, pulling delicately at a stray string. Her nervousness over her father's meeting with Miss Penny was understandable. I sought to reduce her fears to nothing but coals.

"Upon my word, Fran, do not fret over your father and his betrothed. Is that what troubles you, dear friend?"

"Yeah, I guess," Fran said, breaking the string off in its entirety. "It's just . . . "

"Just what, dear Fran? I am your bosom friend, to whom you can spill the depths of your heart and I will not speak it, even unto death."

She smiled. "I know, Polly. It's just that . . . this is all kind of hard for me."

"Hard for you? But Fran, how?"

Her face flushed and she stood, pacing the floor. "How? Well, my mom left us, Polly, remember? And I've had to spend the last three years watching your parents hug and kiss while I've been stuck eating chicken cordon bleu and wishing that maybe someday my dad would love someone—"

"And that time is now, Fran!" I declared. "For tomorrow, your father and Lucy will be united in love's eternal bond! There is no more need to be disheartened."

Fran sighed. "Forget it."

"Forget what, Fran?"

"Nothing." She paused and pulled something from her pocket. It was a picture of a very beautiful woman. "That's her. That's Ruthie Carmichael."

"Really?" I arched my shapely eyebrow and studied the photograph. She was endowed with a face shaped like a heart, large green eyes, and coal-black hair. "She resembles an animal from the feline race, I'm afraid." Fran's face fell downcast at once. "But still," I continued, "though the lady, if that is what she may be, is not equal in beauty to Miss Lucy Penny, her eyes are sufficient enough and her smile appears to be honest."

"Yeah, and she seems really nice, too, Polly."

I handed her back the picture. "Yes, you mentioned that just yesterday."

"I actually really like her. She makes my dad happy and, I don't know, I just like her."

I fiddled with my dress, disbelief over these words silencing me. "But really, you can't mean it, Fran. You like her more than Lucy? I mean, you hardly know this Ruthie at all!"

"Well, I don't know Lucy either. I've only seen her."

"This is true. But not only have I, your bosom friend, recommended her to you, but you will meet her tomorrow, Fran. Unless of course you want me to cancel the meeting."

Fran shrugged her shoulders. "I thought about that, but I guess it's too late now."

"Indeed. It would not be ladylike or gentlemanly to cancel the arrangement when she is so looking forward to it. And I do not think it wise to sever all connections to Miss Penny. The arrangement for the morrow should be kept, and though I see clearly that you are fond of this Ruthie Carmichael, I think you and your father will find Miss Lucy Penny of much more elegance and kindheartedness."

"All right. But you know, Ruthie's coming in just a few days. I guess my dad wanted her to come as soon as she could," Fran said.

"Heavens," I declared, wiping my brow with my handkerchief. "How time steals away when in the midst of bringing lovers together. Believe me, Fran," I said, grasping her hand, "though I adore my task, I do not wish its trial upon you. But do not fret! I am fully convinced in both my heart and my soul that

Miss Penny and your dearest father are a match the very angels in heaven ordained before time began." I glanced at my pocket watch and arose. "But no more of this. I have it all under control. Until then, dear Fran, would you care to accompany me to the beach, where we shall see Mr. Nightquist and Miss Wiskerton unite together in love's perfect harmonic accord?"

She shrugged her shoulders. "Yeah, sure."

We departed thence, and arrived at the beach to find dear Mr. Nightquist silhouetted against the setting sun, attempting to tame an unruly kite. A blanket lay on the sand behind him, surely meant for he and Miss Wiskerton to dine upon.

My heart leapt in my chest.

"He has come, as I knew he would. Such a faithful man the world has never seen," I declared from our cozy spot beneath the creaking planks of the boardwalk. I sought the cover of darkness so as not to distract the couple, but rather observe them.

Mr. Nightquist began to unravel the long white tether attached to the kite and looked about him.

"Where is Miss Wiskerton?" Fran asked from her post beside me.

"She will be along, I promise you." And like a vision,

though a large one, Miss Wiskerton emerged into the soft evening light in a white dress that gently caressed the soft sand at her feet.

Fran and I watched, neither of us uttering a word at this sacred moment.

They shook hands cordially and Miss Wiskerton bowed her head shyly and held out the dish that contained the chicken Marsala. I imagined the words, "Dear Miss Wiskerton, how lovely you look this summer's eve. My heart jumps in delight at this moment."

The flying of the elegant kites began, and my heart joined them, soaring in the sky. But alas, I was torn away from the scene by Fran's earnest tugging on my arm. "Come on, Polly. I think we can go now."

"Just a moment longer, perhaps? A more handsome couple the world has never seen. Don't you agree, Fran?"

"Yeah. But it's almost dinnertime, and I told Dad I'd be back. Besides, I thought I heard the bell from your house ringing."

I grabbed her hands and giggled. "Of course, my dearest, you are the voice of reason. I am grateful to you for keeping me upon the ground, for surely I would fly up into the clouds any moment. The lovers are well, and I must attend to other matters on this most glorious night."

Upon arriving at my small cottage, I plucked a single lily from the garden and swept into the kitchen, placing the fragrant flower in a thin, delicate vase and setting it in the middle of the dining table. Mama sat beside Papa, and Clementine gazed out into the evening sky, her spirits much improved.

The moment was one of pure bliss, with everything right and beautiful in the world. I let my dainty hands caress the flower's velvety petals. "Is it not gorgeous? Ah, what a full and magical day I have had. Isn't each new day as new and sparkly as a diamond, as perfect and innocent as newfound love?"

Clementine's fork dropped to her plate, startling me out of my reverie.

"Put a cork in it, Polly," she said, dabbing at her moistened eyes.

Her tone startled me, since I was quite sure she was most excited about the evening when we would relive times gone by together. "I am sorry, dearest Clementine. Are you still in the abyss of wounded love? For remember, in just two evenings, we will have so much fun that you will forget all about the boring boy who has laid waste to your heart."

She parted her lips to speak but was interrupted by the telephone ringing, which she grabbed with much eagerness.

Dearest Edward already offering words of love and adoration?

"Hey, Clint," she whispered, and then tucked the telephone between her shoulder and ear and left the room.

I arched my brows at the sound of Clint's name. I really had hoped that I had heard the last of him. "Clint?" I directed my questioning look to Papa. "I thought we were rid of him."

"Yeah, I guess they broke up. They've been talking on and off all afternoon."

I dropped my own fork upon the porcelain plate and stood up. "I . . . I'll be right back." There was no time for explanations. I needed to hear Clementine and Clint's conversation at once.

"Just a second, Polly," Mama called from her place at the table. "What were you and Clementine planning to do in a few days?"

"Well, I was hoping to add cheer to her heart by

getting Macko's pizza and collecting seashells as we did when we were younger."

Mama nodded her head. "I know you've been missing Clementine, Polly, but she's growing up, and so are you. You two are sisters, and that'll never change, but things are a little different right now, and I just hope you don't get your hopes up."

The words stung my heart but a little, for I pushed them out of my mind. "Thank you, dear Mama. But I assure you that just like Jane Bennet, Clementine is in need of her sister in these hours of need. Now, if you will excuse me."

Mama smiled. "Really, Polly, I think she just needs some time to work it out with Clint."

I reached down and squeezed her hand in my own. "Thank you, Mama, but really, I am afraid I am quite persuaded on this subject and will not change my mind."

She sighed and shrugged her shoulders. "All right, Polly."

I left the kitchen, tiptoed lightly up the stairs, and took a cup from the bathroom. Placing the open end against Clementine's door, I pressed my ear to the other and listened intently.

"In two nights? Why so long? I'll cancel whatever I need to. . . . All right," Clementine said, and sniffled. "I miss you, too. I'll be at Macko's and we'll talk."

But that was when she and I were going to renew the bonds of sisterly friendship!

Surely this was a mistake. She would never treat me like something to be tossed so easily away, especially over the likes of Clint.

The phone clicked off and I made a hasty retreat to the lavatory and turned the faucet on so that I would not draw suspicion.

Her door opened, and I emerged from the bathroom. "Was that Clint?" I asked.

She smiled, the first hint of joy I had seen on her face the entire day. "Yep, we're gonna meet up and talk, not tomorrow night, but the next night." She sighed and whispered, "Everything will work out."

"But, dearest Clementine, surely you haven't forgotten about you and I going out on that evening?" I watched her face for some sign of remembrance but found none. My heart ached inside me. "Clemmy, you said we could go and get pizza and eat it at the beach and then collect seashells or something. You promised!"

She rolled her eyes in a manner that was quite

unattractive, especially considering the fact that she was backing out of her commitment to her own dear sister.

"Come on, Pol. I need to talk to him. Besides, I don't remember promising anything or even agreeing to it. We can do that another time."

And at that she brushed past me and down the stairs. "Clemmy!" I wailed after her. "You said we would! You're so...so mean!" And then I retired to my bedroom, allowing the door to slam extra hard behind me as a sign of my wounded heart.

I fell upon my bed in a fit of tears and did not even attempt to dab at my nose when I felt it begin to run.

How could she? Did being a sister mean nothing to her? Did all our memories mean nothing? Did our sisterly bond produce no love or affection between us?

I cried harder at the thought that our bond would forever be broken and she would be lost to me forever. I did not try to suppress the tears from coming, for they would not have stopped even if I had used all my powers to restrain them.

"How could you?" I said aloud.

Clint.

Most likely this was all Clint's doing. He probably persuaded her to break all commitments with me. The great beast was once more a barrier between sisters, and Clementine was ruining a chance at true love with Edward. "Indeed," I said aloud, wiping my stinging nose with a handkerchief and rubbing my burning eyes. "I will not let him ruin our sisterly bond." And then I thought upon Edward's arrival in the morning, for surely he would help make all things right once more. This thought comforted me a little and hope renewed itself inside me. "I truly hope that dear Edward's words will awaken Clementine's heart to his gentlemanly qualities and the eternal love that is to be had with him."

Because if not, I must plan a different course of action.

chapter sixteen

In Which Things Go Slightly Awry and I Am Pursued Further

The cheery sun beckoned me awake, as did the unfortunate scent of burning sugar. I arose at once and found myself drawn to the early morning dawn and the quiet solitude of the empty beach. The previous night was painful, yet I would not let go of hope.

I slipped into my pale-blue sundress and fastened my straw hat underneath my chin with the silky ribbon. Edward would surely not arrive so early, and I was in need of an awakening of the mind and heart that only the sea could provide. Thus I slipped by Clementine, who was uttering curses at a rather large bowl of batter.

I would return in time to offer Edward a most glorious selection of pastries, but I knew that I was in need of the sound of the surf to sink deep into my being and prepare me for a new day of love in the making.

Outside the salty breeze tousled my hair, and I listened with rapture to the music of the birds crooning from the treetops. Once by the shore, I stooped upon the sand and plucked a smooth seashell from the shallow waves. Then I wrote upon the sand in beautiful script:

Clementine and Edward

Mr. Fisk and Miss Lucy Penny

Mr. Nightquist and Miss Wiskerton

And then I sat by the names, committing them to the ocean as the tide swept them to the place where the sea's secrets are kept.

"What are you doing out this early, Polly girl?"

"Huh?" I jumped, startled by the sound of a deep voice from behind me. I looked up into the jovial face of Mr. Nightquist. He stood with one hand clutching a spool of string, the other a most beautiful and elegant kite. I stood. "My dear Mr. Nightquist, you quite startled me!"

"Sorry, Polly. I didn't want to interrupt you, but I thought I'd say hello."

"Indeed, I'm glad you did." I gestured to the kite he held fast in his hand. "That one is beautiful indeed."

He nodded and looked down. "It belonged to Miriam, my wife. If you think I'm good at flying kites, you should have seen her. She could really make 'em soar."

"I am sure she could. I only wish that I had been acquainted with the beauty of character that I am sure she possessed." I looked down at the waves of the ocean tickling the sand on the shore. "And may I ask how your lovely evening with the elegant Miss Wiskerton fared?" I gazed down at the shell in my hand, not wanting to sound as eager for every minute detail as I now was.

He smiled. "Good. She hasn't gotten kite flying just yet, but she wants to learn. And she's quite the cook, I'll admit. I'm giving her another lesson this evening."

Could it be? Were his cheeks blushing with anticipation? "I am so pleased, Mr. Nightquist. A more devoted lady no one could find."

"Yeah," he said.

"And how do you think your dear Melissa Anne and her family will view any developments with the elegant Miss Wiskerton?" Though I knew Melissa Anne to be very sympathetic and romantic, I was not sure if she would approve of her father loving another.

He fumbled with the kite, most likely caught up in

thoughts of his fair maiden. "Well, it's not like there's anything serious between Eugenia May and me yet, but actually, I think Missy would be happy. She's been trying to set me up with someone for years, but I just never felt ready. Who knows if I'm ready now? But for some reason, lately I've been feeling like Miriam would actually like it if I loved again, so I'll follow her lead."

"Really? So you've tried to ask her what she thinks? That's so sweet!" I declared, unable to contain my wonder at this new thought. Could it be that he was seeking her counsel this very morning?

"Sure. Miriam was always the one that I turned to for advice, and I'm not about to reject her judgment now."

"Wow," I said, then composed myself. "Mr. Nightquist, that is just so gentlemanly and noble of you!"

"Well, I don't know about that, but I think she's happy for me."

"Good. And I am most thankful she is leading you to this, Mr. Nightquist, for if anyone deserves to be happiest in this life, it is you... and myself, of course, as well as my sister, my dear parents, and of course Fran and her father. But I am tending to those as we speak." I squeezed his hand in mine and bid him farewell. "There are many deliveries to be made this summer morn, so I must be off. Have a lovely evening with Miss Wiskerton."

"Polly?" Mr. Nightquist called after me. "Miss Wiskerton mentioned the delicious pastries I'd given her the past few mornings. She was very grateful. I don't suppose you know anything about them?" He raised one eyebrow in a suspicious manner, though I could tell his expression meant no malice.

Words fumbled inside my head, so I offered him a ladylike smile.

"Well, I suppose you can keep delivering them, though I always like to pay for my purchases. And I think I can take things from here. I might've been out of the game for a while, but I still got it in me." He winked and I waved, relieved that he was not angry with me for working in secret.

Edward was just entering the bakery when I arrived at home, and I was able to sneak undetected through the back door. I had lingered too long at the sea, and now looked around at the carnage that Clementine had made of the muffins. Indeed, at that moment she was poking at a tray of blackened croissants that resembled misshapen pancakes.

"I think there is a customer out front, Clementine," I said, dumping the croissants into the trash can and handing her a tray of Danishes Mama must have made the previous night. "You better go take care of him," I said, and then I pushed her through the doors and into the bakery.

I listened intently at the door and managed to find a sliver through which to see what was taking place.

"Hey, Clementine," Edward said, most gallantly, I must say.

"Hi," she said, most unaffected. Was there hope for my dear sister? "What can I get you?"

"Well, I guess I'll take one of those Danishes. They look good."

Clementine plopped one on a plate and handed it to him. Then she took his money without even gazing into his eyes!

Was all lost?

"I heard that you . . . you weren't doing so good."

She looked up and smiled. "Did Polly tell you that?" She shot a harsh glance toward the door and I cringed. "Well, yesterday wasn't the best day I've had, but today should be better. Thanks for asking."

He smiled. "Sure. Well, I can go with you two to get pizza if you would still like. I was able to switch with someone."

Again Clementine focused her malicious gaze at

me. "Actually, we're not going after all, so you're off the hook."

The pain over this broken commitment sprung up fresh inside me, but I refused to allow the tears to come at this moment.

He shrugged. "Oh, okay. Well, I better go. I'll take the Danish with me." He set the plate on the counter and started for the door. "I'll see you around."

"Sounds good," Clementine said, and began wiping the countertop.

Ugh.

It seemed my sister was determined to ruin any chance at love that she had.

More extreme measures had to be taken.

With this thought heavy upon my mind, I took up the morning's deliveries with a sigh. The pleasant ride to Miss Wiskerton would hopefully bring to my heart a fresh new idea for uniting my sister and Edward. And so I set out for that woman's abode at once. Though Mr. Nightquist had stated he could "take things from here," I still felt that my involvement was essential in case things should fall apart.

Miss Wiskerton lay reclined upon her lawn chair as I stopped and leaned my bicycle against her gate.

"Good morning, Miss Wiskerton," I said, opening

the latch with a click and stepping on her small walkway. She sat up upon her dimpled elbows and lowered her sunglasses down upon her nose to gaze upon me in a prim manner.

"Hello, Polly. Is your sister at the oven again this morning?"

I sighed. "I am afraid that is so. I hope the scent has not caused you too much discomfort."

She waved me away and reclined again on the chair. "Nothing you can do, I suppose."

"Yes, I suppose not. Though in the fall, when she is once again engaged in the trials and tribulations of high school, the pollution she causes will diminish." I stepped forward, receiving a menacing growl from Jack the Nipper. "I have come to deliver another tart from your devoted Mr. Nightquist."

"Oh, really?" She sat up and reached for the bag. "You know he taught me how to fly a kite last night?"

I nodded. "And he said you were a dream to behold, your silhouette upon the setting sun."

"Well, the man practically strangled me with the rope from one of those blasted kites and then it dive-bombed me." She lifted up her arm and pointed to a small brown splotch on her arm. "I bruise very easy and that's what that kite of doom did to me!"

I felt my cheeks redden. Dear Mr. Nightquist thought their evening together a dream, yet she thought quite differently upon the matter.

I had to salvage their love before they were pulled asunder!

"Upon my word, his heart would break if he knew the pain caused you by one of his kites. On the contrary, he adored the culinary concoction you brought and looks forward at this moment to another rendezvous to take place this very evening. I believe he even likened you to the elegant Jane Bennet."

"Really?" She opened the box containing the tart and nibbled at the flaky crust. "Yes, I agreed to meet him, though this is his last chance. I want to live past the age of fifty-three."

"And I'm sure you will. He and you together, living in love's eternal bliss." I went back along the walkway and through the small gate, hoping that my words had soothed her troubled mind. "I must be off, Miss Wiskerton. I wish upon you a most pleasant day."

"Hmm."

And as I continued with the rest of the deliveries for that morning, the love of Miss Wiskerton and

Mr. Nightquist preoccupied my every thought. That evening I would need to intercede on their behalf. Perhaps with scented candles upon the sand, and an array of savory delights to encourage the budding romance.

Yes, I was certain that this was the current course I must take in order to ensure a romance between the two lovers.

I returned home after completing my deliveries and reclined upon my bed. With Lucy and Mr. Fisk's meeting just hours away, and the two other romances—that of Mr. Nightquist and that of Clementine—pressing upon me, I sought wisdom in Jane Austen's elegant words.

But just as I found myself sweeping across the floors of Pemberley the telephone rang. I lifted it to my ear, expecting my dearest friend to be on the other line.

"Can I talk to Polly?" a young man's voice said into my ear.

"This is she. With whom am I speaking?"

"It's Brad. Brad Baker."

"Why... Bradley. I was not expecting your call. How... how are you?" I asked politely, for a lady must be cordial to even the unwanted suitor.

"Good. I'm leaving to go and visit my dad next week and was just calling to see if you wanted to go to Macko's sometime before I leave. I'll buy."

My heart fluttered. Was this really—? I was being asked out for the first time in my life! Heat rose into my cheeks, and I could hardly contain the excitement that bubbled up inside me. I had only dreamed of this moment before now! This was not merely a telephone call about his family history. This was a date!

Bradley continued. "We won't be able to get a whole lot of pizza or Coke, but I have enough for both of us."

"But of course," I said, suppressing my excitement that almost became a giggle. For any gentleman would pay for the lady upon which he set his heart and affections. I was glad that Mr. Baker was refined enough to know this.

"Great, do you want to go tonight?"

I coughed delicately into my handkerchief. "Tonight? Whatever do you mean, sir?"

"Well, you just said, 'But of course.' So how does tonight sound?"

Really, I could hardly think straight, this being the first time I had been asked out on a real date—a real date!—in the course of my entire life, yet still I knew I could not. Not at the moment. "Upon my word, I am indeed sorry, Brad, for the miscommunication. I . . . I have no intention of meeting with you tonight."

I was met with silence and regretted the tone in which I had spoken to him. Surely he was unsuitable for myself, but a kind young man I could not deny.

"I offer you my apolo—"

"Oh, don't worry, Polly. I know that girls like to play hard to get sometimes. But I won't give up, okay?"

Was the gentleman serious? "I am sure, dear Brad, that I do not—"

"I'll call you tomorrow." And the telephone clicked into silence.

I sat upon my bed pondering the conversation that had just taken place. It was just like dear Elizabeth Bennet and Mr. Collins, the unwanted suitor who attempted to push his affections upon her.

And I could see clearly that Mr. Brad Baker, like Mr. Collins, would not give up easily, and I would be forced to use firm words to dissuade him.

Ah, in addition to excitement beyond words, to be admired so intensely did have its problems indeed.

The telephone rang again, and my heart pounded

within my chest as I imagined Brad unable to withhold declaring his sentiments once again.

I allowed the telephone to continue ringing, but my suitor was quite determined, and he called two more times, forcing me to answer.

"Please, Brad, I cannot meet with you. I must assure you that I do not hold the same feelings for you as you—"

"Polly?"

My words ceased momentarily as I came to realize that it was not my unwanted beau, but instead my bosom friend. "Fran? My dearest friend? My apologies for speaking thus to you, but I have had a most distressing conversation with—"

"Tell me later, Polly. You gotta come over quick!" Fran said in a most terrifying manner.

"Oh my gosh! What's wrong?" I sought to compose myself in her time of trial. "What is it, my beloved friend?"

"Just come over now!"

And at that, I departed hence.

chapter seventeen

In Which Terror Strikes Fran's Home and My Suitor Calls . . . Again

The scene unfolding at the home of my dearest and truest of friends was one of complete chaos and terror. A large man was in the process of throwing his massive fist against the Fisks' front door in a manner that was not becoming to a gentleman at all. Indeed, the language he spoke was also not appropriate for ladies such as myself and Fran to hear.

I rode to the backyard to avoid the beast and discarded my bicycle on the ground. Relieved to find that Mr. Fisk had not yet relocated the spare key from its secret location underneath the loose brick to the right of the back door, I quickly entered their home.

Fran met me, her eyes brimming with silvery tears and her cheeks flushed red with anxious worry.

I scanned the room once I was assured that she was sound of body. "Where is your father?"

"He's on the phone."

"Alerting the authorities of this madman's rage, I am sure." Convinced that we were not all about to be bludgeoned, I turned to her and clasped her hands in mine. "Now please, my dearest Fran, tell me all."

"Well, the guy came up to the house about fifteen minutes ago. He came to the door and asked if my dad was there."

"And that is when your home came under siege." But who could the great brute be? Whom had Mr. Fisk angered so?

"Stay away from my girl!" he yelled in the midst of a string of the most ghastly profanities.

The scene became, at once, all too clear to me.

Mr. Fisk was wooing the computer woman, Miss Ruthie Carmichael, who was otherwise betrothed to a ruthless suitor with a jealous temper. Seeking a harbor in her desperation, Miss Carmichael sought a compassionate man and was united in cyberspace with Mr. Fisk. But one night, as Miss Carmichael sat conversing with Mr. Fisk on the telephone, their intimate conversation was heard and the man's jealous rage burst into flames. And so he lit upon Mr. Fisk to enact his vengeance.

"Polly?! Come on, you have to tell them this is all a big mistake!"

Fran stood before me, her hands clasped as in prayer. Mr. Fisk held in his grip a golf club—his chosen weapon of defense.

"As you wish, beloved Fran. My dear Mr. Fisk," I said. "Though I do not like this task, I must tell you that Miss Ruthie Carmichael's vengeful suitor is at your door. I hope the authorities are on their way. I am sure he is quite dangerous when in his rage."

"Ruthie? Polly, what are you talking about?" Fran stood, her hands upon her hips. "It isn't Ruthie. He's saying something about Luc—"

"Please, David. Stop this now!" a delicate woman's voice called from outside.

The lady's voice sounded so very familiar to my ears. Could it be that I knew this Miss Carmichael?

"Stay out of this, Luce," the low voice said firmly. "You're my girl, and I'm not going to let any fancy talker steal you away."

"But please, David."

Fran grasped my arm and squeezed so that I feared developing a bruise. "Not *Ruthie*, Polly. He's saying *Lucy,* as in *Lucy Penny.*" She said these last words through clenched teeth so that Mr. Fisk could not hear.

The name of Mr. Fisk's intended drained all color from my rosy complexion, and I felt the ground beneath my feet swirl. "Oh, dear," I declared, certain that a swoon was upon me.

"Don't you dare faint, Polly Madassa," Fran said, squeezing my arm ever tighter. "You got us into this mess and you need to get us out."

Could it be? Could it be that the one lady worthy of the honorable Mr. Fisk was involved with such a beast? Had I been deceived? I banished the thought. I had seen in her elegant eyes the admiration and adoration of her suitor—Mr. Fisk. "I cannot believe it is she. I must see with my own eyes."

"All right," Fran said, dragging me quite indelicately by the arm to the window. "See, there she is."

I peered through the lattice and saw that indeed, much to my dismay and the breaking of my heart, it was true. There stood Miss Penny, elegant in a long lavender gown and straw hat, her curls cascading down her shoulders. She was prepared for the tea. Perhaps this . . . *David* had followed her in secret to this very home, suspecting that her affections had turned to another.

"What is going on, girls?" Mr. Fisk's voice was stern behind our backs.

And in the brief moment upon which I turned toward my bosom friend's father, I felt a deep loss and hopelessness at the situation. I had failed Mr. Fisk and my dearest Fran. Yet furthermore, they were now in grave danger. The tears that threatened to fill my eyes over this lost romance were suppressed by the chilling thought of harm, which overwhelmed me.

"Come on, Polly," Mr. Fisk spoke softly, though with a hint of urgency. "It's all right. But you have to tell me what's going on before he breaks the door down."

Fran wrapped her comforting arm around me, squelching my tears. I took a life-giving breath and was about to repent, when the horrible yelling ceased and instead the delicate voice of Miss Penny called through to us.

"Mr. Fisk. My name is Lucy Penny. I am very sorry for this. Please come out and talk with me so that we can get this whole thing resolved."

Mr. Fisk walked promptly to the door, with Fran and me clutching his shirttails in an effort to rescue him should he need our aid.

"Be ever so careful, Mr. Fisk. A lover scorned is a terrible force," I whispered.

He turned to me and raised his eyebrows with a questioning gaze, then opened the door. "Miss Penny? I'm George Fisk. Can you—?"

But dear Mr. Fisk was not able to complete his sentence, for David was not to be restrained and lunged for my friend's father.

"Stop!" I wailed as loudly as any young lady in such dire circumstances would and succeeded in stopping the assault for the moment.

And those around me grew quiet and still.

"Just stop. It's all my fault... I mean, it is I—I who has brought this unfortunate situation to fruition."

Fran smacked her hand upon her alabaster forehead.

"What are you talking about, Polly?" Mr. Fisk asked, his arms still poised as if defending a blow.

"Surely Miss Penny knows who I am."

"Of course. This is the girl who brought me the flowers and the pastry from Mr. Fisk."

"But I never sent anyone—" Mr. Fisk broke in.

And all at once, all who were present became my attentive audience.

"Indeed, it was I," I said. "Fearful, Mr. Fisk, of your involvement with this woman whom you have met on that computer, I persuaded your dearest daughter to allow me to find you a suitable, elegant, and beautiful woman, one worthy of your affections. Miss Lucy

Penny was the woman whom I found, and to whom you gave a lovely bouquet of flowers and a most delicious pastry."

"So it wasn't actually him who sent me the flowers?" Miss Penny asked.

With eyes downcast, I shook my head no.

"Or invited me to tea?"

Again, I shook my head.

She laughed a most hearty and forgiving laugh that instantly lightened my soul. "Well, I have to say, you were quite good, Polly. David and . . ." She looked over at the man, who resembled every bit a dunce. "We've gone on a few dates over the past few months, and well, I didn't think he was very serious about me. Now, however . . ." She gazed into his eyes that were a rather dull blue compared to dear Mr. Fisk's.

"Course I'm serious about you, Luce. I just haven't gotten much of a chance to show you."

And those words, however unromantic they were, caused the two to lock in a lover's embrace that was not nearly as beautiful as I imagined Mr. Fisk and Miss Penny's union would be.

David held out his hand and Mr. Fisk shook it tentatively. "Sorry about all the noise and the misunderstanding. I hope I didn't scare you all too bad."

Mr. Fisk sighed. "It's all right."

"At least now Luce knows how much I'd like to go out with her."

At that moment a police car arrived on the scene. However, they did not linger long once they were assured that peace had been restored. The couple then departed on the wings of love.

I sighed. Though this ending was not what I had envisioned or desired, love had indeed prevailed, and in that my heart rejoiced.

I turned to Fran and sighed. "Though I think your father was a much better match for the lovely lady, I suppose David may have some admirable qualities about him, however small they may be."

"All right, girls," Mr. Fisk said ever so sternly, and I recalled the fact that Mr. Fisk was most likely much perturbed about the situation. He placed his firm hands upon our shoulders. "You two, in the house, now."

Fran and I followed him inside like prisoners of war. What would be our fate? Servants for a fortnight? Made to scrub the floors as payment for our trespasses?

We sat upon the couch and awaited our judgment.

I glanced up at Mr. Fisk as he stood by the hearth, leaning on it like a figure from a classic book. If there had been a pipe in his mouth, he'd have looked very distinguished indeed.

"So, what is all this?" he asked. "Flowers from me, pastries from me? It seems like I've been pretty busy."

I placed a gentle hand on Fran's. I would lay down my own life for the honor of my bosom friend. "It was I. Your dearest daughter is not to blame. That rests on my own head. It was my idea. I only sought to bring you to a union that was sure to be one from a dream."

"And in this matchmaking dream did you see me get punched in the nose?"

"Of course not, dear sir! Nothing of the sort. If you speak of Miss Lucy's suitor, I am still convinced that the match will not work in the end and if you wish, I will keep a watchful eye on—ouch."

Fran pinched my arm, and I was quite sure a bruise was in the process of forming on my delicate skin at that very moment.

Mr. Fisk sighed. "No thanks, Polly. That's nice that you want to help, but I've already found a wonderful woman, who is visiting in just—"

"A few days. Yes, Fran has told me about this... *Ruthie Carmichael*, but, since you do not know this woman, I find the situation very suspicious and possibly dangerous."

Mr. Fisk scratched his noble chin. "But really, you didn't know much about that Lucy Penny either, and that nearly got us killed."

"That was purely a . . . a misunderstanding. I know it was presumptuous of me. But I have had successful experience at matchmaking." I looked at Fran, hoping she did not bring up the fact that it was of a canine nature.

"You have, have you?"

"Yes, sir. And you have to admit, if Miss Penny weren't . . . weren't already spoken for, she would be someone who would have suited your heart's desire."

He shrugged his shoulders. "Maybe, maybe not. She seems nice, but beyond that I don't know her at all. This 'computer woman,' as you refer to her, is completely real and honest and, well, she's wonderful."

I let out a sigh. Though the way he said these words was ever so romantic and sincere, I was still not convinced that Ruthie Carmichael was a woman to be trusted. The Fisks' previous situation involving Internet communication gave me much reason to doubt, and I was inwardly shocked that it did not seem to trouble Mr. Fisk's soul in the least.

"So enough of this matchmaking, girls, okay? I'm a big boy and can take care of myself. And don't worry," Mr. Fisk said, placing a loving hand upon Fran's head. "I'd never make any decisions without talking with you first, Fran. You'll always be my number-one girl."

Fran smiled.

"Now that I've survived that ordeal with all my limbs still in place, I'm going to go to my office and get some work done."

He placed a delicate kiss on top of Fran's elegant forehead before retiring to his office.

Fran turned to me once the door had clicked closed. "Polly, I can't believe you didn't know she was seeing someone else. Lucky for me, he didn't ground me for life!"

She was angered. I saw it in the way her chin trembled ever so slightly in a manner that was quite exquisite, while the depth of her feelings moved me to compassion. I made a mental note to practice this gesture at home.

I reached for her hand. "Please accept my apologies, dear Fran. I did not know of this prior relationship of Miss Penny's, and feel equally deceived that she had not been honest with me from the first."

She rolled her eyes and sighed. "It's all right, I guess.

But it's over, okay? Ruthie's coming in just a few days and, Polly, she's really nice. I think you'd love her."

I shook my head, my curls swishing gently around my face. "This is not over in the least, dearest Fran. I cannot leave you, the dearest friend of my heart, or your father, alone in this hour. I fear that I care for you too greatly, and maybe that is where I am at fault. But forward I must proceed, and I promise that I shall find for your father a woman of impeccable manners, beauty, and elegance who will melt his heart and bring you all the happiness that you so richly deserve."

"But Dad told us to stop. You can't, Polly. He'll kill me." Fran looked quite desperate.

"But I must, Fran. I know you are not as familiar in the ways of love as I am, but it is for the best. Your father seems to like this Ruthie Carmichael very much. But how much, I ask, and is this love for real? That is what we must determine. By introducing him to another beautiful woman, either his love for Ruthie will falter and their connection will end, or it will cause his love for her to increase."

Her eyebrows furrowed. "So, you're saying that we set my dad up again so that he knows for sure that he really likes Ruthie?"

"Indeed, I am."

She shrugged. "I guess that makes sense. But he'll have our heads if he finds out."

"We will not let him know what we are planning. The woman will arrive as a friend of ours and conveniently meet your father over a tea that we will give. Therefore your father will not suspect a thing from us."

"Okay, but Polly, if he doesn't fall for this new girl, then all the matchmaking is over, okay?"

"You have my solemn vow as your bosom friend."

But as I departed, I was quite sure that the woman I found would surely become Mr. Fisk's one true love, the one who would complete him. "I will speak with you tonight, Fran!" I called back to her, waving my handkerchief in the air to bid her good-bye.

But as dusk fell like dew upon the grass, I had yet to find a woman for Mr. Fisk.

I had met an elegant lady sitting in Fran's and my spot beneath the Old One in the Haven of Heaven. I approached her as she sat underneath the boughs, book in hand, whilst the sun glinted off her golden hair. But after a minute or two I found that she had only just begun college, and was therefore not suitable for Mr. Fisk (who himself could have been her father).

Another woman I found walking along the beach. Her hair was speckled with strands of silvery gray, though her face bore no wrinkles of the aged. I followed her for a ways, and then was dismayed to find five children running toward her and calling her "Mommy!" Though I knew that Mr. Fisk adored the young, to once again be burdened with the trials of toddlerhood is a fate that I wish upon no one who has already escaped it. Especially after seeing the unpredictable behavior of Mr. Nightquist's grandson, Charles.

And so I retreated home, defeated in spirits, though attempting to be hopeful. After supper I retired to my bedroom to contemplate a bit more where I might find such a lady as would be suitable.

Once in my bedroom, I collapsed onto my satin comforter and pulled out *Pride and Prejudice* and *Anne of Green Gables*, letting the words soak into my being, something that always aided me in times of trial.

A knock on my door awoke me from romantic dreams of Mr. Fisk and the woman who would fulfill his heart's longing as Elizabeth Bennet had fulfilled Mr. Darcy's.

"You may enter."

My dearest sister swept inside, a sly smile upon her lips. Oh, dear! I still had not determined how I was to keep Clint and Clementine from meeting with one another. But though instantly troubled, I composed myself with grace. "Yes, Clementine?"

"There's someone at the door for you."

"Heavens, I did not even hear the ring of the doorbell, so consumed was I in my own pensive thoughts."

"It's a boy," she said, causing my heart to tremble in my breast.

"Oh, no! It must be Brad!" I grasped my sister's hand in mine. "Dearest Clementine, you must save me from having to speak with him. I fear he will not be dissuaded from pursuing me."

She laughed. "You don't like him? He seems like a nice guy."

"I can vouch for his character, though I abhor the thought of him as a suitor for myself. Please, Clementine, tell him—" My mind was empty of thoughts. "Tell him . . . tell him that I am in the throes of sickness and that . . . that I am not expected to recover for quite some time. That should convince him to leave me be, and perhaps he will pursue another girl."

She laughed again. "All right. But only this time. If he comes back, you need to say it to him yourself, okay?"

I nodded and fell upon my knees. "My dearest sister, I thank you from the depths of my being for this favor that you do me. You are indeed—"

"Save it, Polly," she said, and shut my door.

But I feared to move from this spot, even though my eyes longed to see his reaction to such news about my health. It was only when the door shut below that I heard Clementine walk lightly up the stairs and knock once more on my door. "He left this for you," she said, and handed me a box that was wrapped in such bright pink paper that I feared for my eyesight.

She left me alone and I unwrapped the gift to find a delicate golden clock. The sight was breathtaking as I drank in the elegant curves of the miniature timepiece. I brought the face to my ear and smiled at the rhythmic *tick tock*, *tick tock* that pulsed inside it.

It was a grand gift indeed, and one that I was tempted to accept. But alas, I knew I could not. Accepting his gift would be accepting him, and I would not give him false hope.

I could not.

But the time was drawing late, so I set the

beautiful clock upon my nightstand and turned off the light, allowing myself one night of enjoyment of the gift before I returned it to Mr. Baker.

And indeed, I slept well under its watchful, golden eye.

chapter eighteen

In Which I Find Another Suitable Woman for My Bosom Friend and Devise a Plan to Save My Dearest Sister

Upon finishing breakfast the next morn, I departed with a basket laden with pastries for empty stomachs, and plans of love for yearning hearts.

Passing by Miss Wiskerton's home, I was reminded of the romantic evening she and Mr. Nightquist surely had had the night before. In all that had happened at Fran's home, I had forgotten that I had wanted to be at the beach to ensure that all would go well with them. I would just have to trust that love had entwined them to each other. For though my heart ached to hear of their blossoming romance, time would not permit me. I had but one day to find the woman that would forever nourish Mr. Fisk's body, mind, and soul.

If a moment allowed, I would call upon the dear lady to hear her thoughts on the previous evening and to accept her gracious thanks for bringing she and dear Mr. Nightquist together.

But the morning did not bode well. Nary a woman I saw was suitable for Mr. Fisk. Many were much too old, others much too young, such that by the early afternoon, as the sun beat down upon my back, I began to despair.

Could it be that I had failed my dearest friend? Would she remain motherless for all eternity, with only her father and her bosom friend as companions?

I imagined my dearest Fran growing older, age lining her delicate face. (All the more likely since she refused to protect her skin with a bonnet.) And because she never had a mother to call her own, vowing her soul into the humble service of the great Virgin Mother. And though it was indeed a romantic destiny, it was not one that I would choose for my bosom friend. And it was that vision that awakened my heart anew. I would continue to search on Fran's behalf.

I must.

"Polly?"

I awoke from my vision to find Mrs. Miller, Fran's former piano teacher, standing before me. Recently divorced, I had thought she was hoping to spend time traveling the world this summer. "Why, Mrs. Miller.

I thought you were taking leave of our town for a month or two. I hope you are well." I offered up a small curtsy.

"Yeah, I thought about it, but decided to stay. And I'm doing really good. Yourself?"

"Very well, thank you. I am reluctant to admit to you that Fran aches for her piano lessons ever so much. I hope your summer thus far has been refreshing to your soul and that you will return to instructing once more."

"Yep, you can tell her that I'll be starting up lessons in the fall and would love to have her. I'm taking the summer off to enjoy myself a bit and, you know, get myself fixed up here and there."

The eyes of my heart were opened at once, and I knew that fate had intervened!

An elegant divorcée with a voice like an angel and fingertips that sang the songs of heaven itself! Love was working its delicate hands to weave a romance the likes of which the world had never seen.

It was she, Mrs. Miller, who would capture Mr. Fisk's heart. Yes, I was certain.

The lovely lady began to walk away, but she stopped when I called to her. "Yes, Polly?"

Words flowed through my soul. "Would you

perhaps—" I hesitated only briefly; my words had to be given lightly, for I did not want to frighten the dear woman. "As you know, Fran's father, Mr. George Fisk, a man of unspeakable character and kindness, is divorced as well. Would you consider joining Mr. Fisk, his daughter, and myself for an elegant dessert tomorrow evening? You can discuss Fran's future as a pianist as well as become better acquainted with one another."

Mrs. Miller wrung her small, dimpled hands, though her eyes betrayed her excitement. "Well, I don't know. I feel like I should be asked by Mr. Fisk or by Fran. Are you sure?"

"Why yes, I am sure. As his daughter's bosom friend, I am like family to Mr. Fisk. Please say that you will do us the honor?"

"I . . . I guess so. Yes, yes I'll go. Thank you very much." Her face glowed with the hope of love.

"Really? That's awesome . . . I am so pleased to hear that, and I will go straightaway to let Fran and her father know of the arrangements. You may join us at seven o'clock."

"I'll see you then."

And we parted ways, Mrs. Miller filled with the

promise of tomorrow, and myself filled with visions of the union of her and Mr. Fisk.

I made my path home, considerably more hopeful in spirit upon the anticipation of the next evening's events. Yet I knew it was most urgent that I also discover when Clementine and Clint were meeting, that I might be prepared to stop their rendezvous.

Mama and Papa were just closing up the bakery when I entered.

"Hey, Polly!" Papa said. "How did the deliveries go?"

"Considerably well," I replied. "Is Clementine about?"

Mama nodded. "I think so. She went out this morning to get a new outfit for her and Clint's 'talk,' but I think she's home now."

Indeed, she was at home, as I found out upon reaching her room. She giggled on the phone and I pressed my ear against the wood, praying that it was not Clint she conversed so happily with.

"Yeah, we're going to talk tomorrow night around eight, I guess. He wants to meet at Macko's, and then I think we'll take the pizza down to the pier, where we can sit and dangle our legs into the water like we did on our first date. I think I'm going to make him some brownies or something, since those are his favorite."

There was a slight pause, and I waited eagerly for her to continue.

"So does he really seem sad? Good. Oh, don't worry, I'll call you and let you know. Thanks, Tracy."

Eight o'clock! I smiled and shut myself in my bedroom. That was enough time in which to put an end to their meeting. Yet how? She had not yet fallen madly in love with Edward, and that gentleman made no great declarations of his love to her. Still, I was convinced that if Clementine could but see Edward as the prince he was, surely her heart and devotion would be his.

Oh, that was it!

I would beseech Edward to save Clementine from Clint tomorrow evening. What lady of quality does not wish her suitor to fight for her honor and attentions? And I had already mentioned to Edward that Clint was a brute, and as a proper English gentleman he would not fail to try and rescue Clementine. Especially if the pizza and drink they were to partake of was said to be... poisoned. Yes, that would be the right course. Edward would, very gallantly, rid them of their dinner, challenge Clint to a duel, and free Clementine from Clint forever. Then Clementine, seeing the love Edward has for her—his willingness to lay down his life for her and treat her as she deserves—would certainly fall into his arms for all eternity.

It was perfect!

I would deliver a pastry to Edward in the morning and ask him this favor, which I was confident he would grant. With my course in this matter determined, I telephoned Fran to let her know of the joyous news of Mrs. Miller.

"Mrs. Miller?" Fran asked. "But she's so . . . so . . . I don't know. She's my piano teacher."

"But Fran, you have always adored her. She is pleasant, with a nice smile and an elegant demeanor. And if your father would not fall madly in love with her, which I find hard to believe, it will serve as a test of your father's love for this Ruthie Carmichael."

She sighed. "All right, Polly. I guess it should work. My dad'll think that she's over to talk about piano lessons."

"Yes, it will be most pleasant, I am sure. Mrs. Miller is an elegant beauty to be sure and the music she plays will trill a song in his heart. Well, I must go, dear Fran.

But I promise to be by your side during the evening's first eye contact between your father and the fair Mrs. Miller."

"All right, Polly. See you tomorrow."

I lay upon my bed and sighed. "Ah, me. Love is in the air."

And after reading my most favorite passages in my most beloved books, I fell into a light sleep.

chapter nineteen

In Which Bradley Continues to Court Me and I Acquire Edward's Help

I was awakened hours later by a light tapping on my windowpane and a low voice whispering on the wind. "Polly? Polly?"

Had I perished in my sleep and become a spirit?

I opened my eyes and searched the darkness only to find the silhouette of a young man outside my window.

I jumped from my bed and reached for an antique candlestick I had acquired on my eighth birthday. "Who are you and why do you haunt me?" I whispered in earnest.

"Polly, it's only me, Brad. Brad Baker."

I rushed to my bedside and pulled the string on my lamp. Indeed it was he, my suitor. Unable to sleep, his soul had brought him to my bedroom window. The thought was romantic enough to cause me to swoon, so I leaned on my dressing table that I might remain grounded. "Why have you come? The hour is late."

"It's not that late," he said, clutching a branch. His hair, tousled in the wind, blew off of his forehead in a manner that was most becoming to him. "I don't even think it's nine yet. I rang the doorbell and your sister told me I should climb this tree if I wanted to talk to you."

Dearest Clementine?! She knew of romance then! I sighed. Yes, surely Edward would win her heart tomorrow night. I gazed at Bradley, perched outside my bedroom window, looking dashing in the moonlight, and my senses at once were lost.

I turned to my persistent suitor. "My dear Bradley, though I am most flattered and overcome by this declaration of love, it is not proper for a young man to be in a lady's bedroom, especially at this hour of night."

"You're going to confess your love? Really? Well, gosh." A smile spread wide across his face, and his braces glinted like silver in the moonlight. Then he grunted and struggled with his hold. "Do you think I could come in for just a second? My arms . . . are getting . . . really tired. I'll just go out the front door . . . if you don't mind."

I sighed. Though I could not imagine such a thing being allowed in Elizabeth Bennet's time, I figured it would be much better than having him fall to the ground to his ultimate demise. "If you must."

And though I was fully clothed, I pulled on my dressing gown as was proper. And as I turned around, I witnessed Bradley jump from the tree to my window and land on my floor with a deafening thud. "Ouch!"

"Oh my gosh! I mean . . . dear me, are you all right? You are not killed, are you?"

Bradley groaned and sat up. His ruddy cheeks were scraped raw, as were his hands from clutching the tree. "No, I think . . . I think I'm fine." He gazed down at his hands. "Do you have a Band-Aid or something?"

"Sure." I ran into the washroom across the hall and came back with a clean basin of water, bandages, and ointment. "Here, let me aid you," I said, imagining myself a nurse, bandaging the wounds of a fallen soldier. He would gaze in my eyes, memorizing my face in his mind. After the war, he would find me, the benefactress of his health. And bending down on one knee he would vow to love me always.

I sighed.

"You all right? I think that's good enough."

I looked up to find I had bandaged Bradley's hand

as well as his arm and shoulder. I felt my cheeks flush under his thankful gaze. "Why yes, I am quite fine. Now let me walk you to the door."

Neither Clementine nor my parents were in sight as I opened the front door and bid him farewell.

"So do you want to go to Macko's sometime?" Bradley asked.

My resolve began to disintegrate at his romantic persistence. "Perhaps, though I fear I cannot answer you this night. There is much that I must do before I might give myself over to your attentive courtship."

He shrugged his shoulders. "All right, Polly. I'll ask you again tomorrow, I guess." And with those parting words, he stepped onto a small scooter and pushed off down the street into the darkness.

Back up in my bedroom I contemplated what had just taken place. Had my heart begun to soften toward the young man? But he was not what I truly desired in a suitor, and I feared that he would never be. Though his gestures were most romantic, surely a bond between us was not meant to be.

But as I lay upon my bed, dreams came in softness and beauty. The prince I often dreamt about was by my bedside. I lay ailing from a fever I had acquired after nursing a sick child back to health, and when the gentleman kissed my alabaster hand, he looked up, and his face was Bradley's.

I found upon the morn my spirit lightened, the dreams of the night having been nourishment for my soul. Mere hours remained before Mrs. Miller would arrive at Fran's home to make all right again and dearest Clementine would be united with Edward.

After selecting a chocolate croissant for Edward and another for Miss Wiskerton, I set upon my duties with a hopeful heart.

When I came to within a short distance of that genteel woman's home, I spied her and came to a halt. Was not that Mr. Nightquist delivering a bouquet of flowers to Miss Wiskerton as she sat reclining on her chair? Was that not Mr. Nightquist petting Jack the Nipper on his tender, furry head?

I hid myself behind foliage and listened.

Miss Wiskerton blushed and smiled, bringing the flowers to her face. "Thank you, Peter. They're beautiful."

"Sure thing." Mr. Nightquist shuffled his feet. He was, indeed, the dearest man. "Do you need anything,

Eugenia May? My shop doesn't open for another hour and I can . . . I can help you out with something around the house if you need."

She touched the flowers with her fingertips. "Oh, I think I'm all right. But why don't you come on in and I'll show you around. Maybe you could come for lunch too?"

Mr. Nightquist assisted her out of the lounge chair. "I can't today. My daughter, Missy, and my grandboy, Charlie, are supposed to meet me for lunch. Maybe—"

"Well, why don't you invite them along? I'd love to get to know them."

I cringed. The visions of Miss Wiskerton meeting the obstinate Charles were not welcome. But I supposed if Mr. Nightquist was to be united in matrimony to Miss Wiskerton, they were bound to meet up eventually.

I offered a prayer up to heaven beseeching any help for Charles to become, at least for an hour, a well-behaved young lad, rather than what he was.

Mr. Nightquist and Miss Wiskerton entered her domain, and I stood. I was thankful that the two lovers did not notice my presence, for I was convinced that interrupting love's work would be a sin most unforgivable.

Knowing that love was blossoming, I set off on the

rest of my deliveries with a heart that was brimming over with delight.

I made my way to the toy shop and found Edward outside.

The sun glinted off the bike he polished like silver armor. I crossed the street, shrouded by a small crowd of people, and stopped at the window of a small bookstore, pretending to gaze at the selections in the window. He could not see me, for his broad, handsome shoulders were toward me. I did not want to seem too eager to see him, or for him to know of my intentions.

I coughed loud enough for him to hear me.

"Polly? Is that you?"

I turned to him, the picture of surprise upon my face. "Why Edward, it is so very good to see you this beautiful morning. I hope that all goes well with the toy industry?"

He slapped the bike. "Well, I think as long as people keep having kids, the toy industry will do just fine. So, is there anything I can do for you today?"

"Actually, I wanted to stop by and say thank you for your kind words to my dear sister. They soothed her beyond words, and for that I offer you this croissant made by her own hands."

He took the croissant and smiled. "Sure. It seemed she was just fine, though, so I'm not sure how much I helped."

"Oh, you did, I assure you." I looked down, fixing a look of despair upon my face. "It is just that she cannot show it."

"Why not?" he said, taking a large bite from the croissant.

"The brute I mentioned to you before. He seems to have a hold on her that is most distressing. And even tonight he has forced her to go out with him. I fear for her safety and for her spirit."

"She should just tell him she doesn't want to go."

"I wish that she could, but it seems that she is too beaten down and filled with despair. If only someone would stand up to Clint and rescue Clementine." I gazed up at his face, but he was concentrating too much on the croissant. I sighed. "I'm sure a gentleman like you would come to her rescue."

He shrugged. "Course. If she really needed it."

I grasped his hand. "Oh, but she does. I have been informed that he plans to poison both her dinner and her beverage with a horrible potion. Please, please, Edward. Help my sister!" And I managed to spring fresh tears to my eyes.

He stopped eating. "This must be serious. I'll help her. Just tell me what time and where and I'll get rid of that guy."

I informed him of the time and the place.

"So you're certain that the pizza and the drink are dangerous?"

I shook my head yes with great solemnity. "Indeed, I am quite certain. He may not mean to kill her, but to cause her sickness I am quite sure." *Heartsickness being the worst of all such poisons*, I inwardly pondered. "Yes, he is a foul beast and not to be trusted." Then I offered thanks on behalf of my entire family. "We are indebted to you as the Bennets were to Mr. Darcy when he acted on their behalf concerning the foul beast Wickham. Thank you, Edward, and Godspeed."

And we parted ways.

From there, I found respite in the Haven of Heaven and proceeded to reread my favorite chapters of *Pride and Prejudice*. I needed to be assured that love doth prevail.

And having read the scene where at last Elizabeth and Mr. Darcy are united in love, I could not help but lean back upon the grass and whisper, "Elizabeth and

Mr. Darcy together at last," into the late-afternoon breeze.

I closed the book, shut my eyes to the world around me, and hugged the book to my breast before pulling my dainty golden clock from the pocket of my dress. I had been reading for hours, and the time was near for Mrs. Miller to arrive at Fran's home.

Yet I was not tired. Rather I was invigorated by the prospects before me.

And as I rode to Fran's home, I couldn't help but enjoy the breeze tousling my hair, the sun sparkling above, and the sight of my pale yellow dress billowing out around me like a cloud at sunset.

chapter twenty

In Which Mrs. Miller Is Greatly Changed and Clementine's Heart Is Hardened Toward Me

I arrived at Fran's home with but moments to spare before Mrs. Miller was to arrive. It seemed that though I had experienced setbacks in my "love in the making," nothing could go amiss this day.

I had, indeed, found my calling in this life.

Fran met me at the door, her face, I could tell, filled with eagerness and excitement. "Is she going to be here soon?"

"Indeed she will, my dearest Fran. And do not fear for the evening. I have the utmost confidence that Mrs. Miller and your dear father will find love kindled between them upon the moment their eyes meet."

"And if not," Fran said, wagging a finger that appeared to have a bit of cordon bleu on it, "he'll probably fall more deeply in love with Ruthie."

"Maybe," I said, and searched the room. "And how is your father, Fran? I do not see him about."

"Oh, he's fine. I told him she's coming to talk about lessons for me. He said that was fine, but he hasn't come out of his office all afternoon."

I was alarmed. "Dear me. We have to get him out of there. Who knows what state he is in? Come, Fran! We do not want Mrs. Miller to be scared at the sight of him."

Mr. Fisk was indeed in a state of disarray. He wore a tropical button-up shirt—buttoned incorrectly so that one side of the shirt hung considerably lower than the other side. His hair was a wild mass on top of his head, and his toes poked out of the plaid slippers adorning his feet.

"But this is what I'm comfortable in. Why do I need to change?"

"Indeed, it does look comfortable, if that is how you describe it," I said. "But the Hawaiian button-up shirt that you are currently wearing is meant for an afternoon at the beach, not for an evening meeting with Fran's piano teacher. Fran and I will find something proper for you to wear."

We left him downstairs while we chose an appropriate shirt and then we brought with us a comb and deodorant, and a bottle of cologne that did not appear to have been opened since its purchase.

He dressed and combed his hair while I gave him a healthy dose of cologne. "You two aren't planning anything I should know about, right? Remember, I said no matchmaking."

"Indeed not, Mr. Fisk. There, you look like quite a handsome gentleman now!"

He smiled. "All right. But really I don't see why I couldn't have just called her on the phone."

"These things are better done in person, Mr. Fisk," I assured him, and then clutched Fran's hand in my own while we awaited Mrs. Miller's arrival.

A full forty-five minutes later, we still sat.

At first I was appalled by her lack of punctuality—it is not ladylike to keep one's hosts waiting.

But after one hour it was clear that something must have gone amiss, and that dear Mrs. Miller had been detained by a horrible accident.

"Oh well, I guess she's not coming," Mr. Fisk said, rising to his feet.

"Please, Mr. Fisk," I said in earnest desperation. "Give the good woman a few moments longer, I beg you."

Just then the doorbell rang out clear and strong, and both Fran and I jumped to our feet.

She had arrived!

I nodded at Mr. Fisk. "Why don't you get the door?" I suggested, helping him through these first minutes. After they beheld each other's eyes, I was sure that no more help would be needed. Love would direct their path.

Fran and I followed but a few steps behind him, eager to behold the moment when they made eye contact with one another.

Mr. Fisk opened the door, blocking dear Mrs. Miller from my view.

"Well, hello, Mrs. Miller. Um, it's good to see you again."

I clutched my bosom friend's hand in my own and smiled at her. Though I could not see them gazing into each other's eyes, I imagined it, and the scene was quite beautiful to behold.

"Come on in."

And in she came.

And yet, this...this could not be! Who was this woman? This was not Mrs. Miller! It could not be. Mrs. Miller wore elegant shirts and nicely tailored pants. She always wore her hair in a neat bun and let the natural beauty of her face shine through.

This woman was quite the opposite... yet... yet there was something familiar about her.

"What happened to her?" Fran whispered earnestly into my ear. "You didn't tell me she looked different."

"Oh, gosh! She didn't yesterday, I promise!" I attempted to compose my own surprise and reassure my dearest friend. "It was but yesterday afternoon when last I saw her and now she looks quite... quite changed."

And indeed she did.

This woman that stood in Fran's home looked nothing like the Mrs. Miller who taught Fran how to play the piano. This woman's hair was roughly the height of a grown calla lily and thick streaks of the whitest blonde stood out like beacons in her dark tower of hair. Her face yesterday had been a delicate shade of honey brown. This evening, it was a shade of orange I had seen only on the face of a chrysanthemum. Thick black eyelashes hung so far over her eyes I could not tell what color her eyes actually were. And there was something about her eyebrows that gave her a look of continual surprise. I had a feeling this was the result of too much plucking and waxing on her part.

She turned toward Fran and I. "Well, hi, Polly! You

like my makeover? It'll make my ex-husband so jealous, don't you think? And Fran, I just can't wait to start teaching you lessons again, though I won't be able to start up until the fall. I've got a few surgeries ahead of me before I can devote time to them again."

"Oh, I didn't know you were divorced. I'm sorry. Are you doing okay?" Mr. Fisk asked with genuine concern.

Mrs. Miller knocked him on the shoulder in a manner unbefitting a woman of good breeding. "Course I am, sweetie. I just want to get a few things fixed up, you know? A little here and a little there and a little . . . well, you know where. You'll want to take a picture of my ex-husband's face when he sees me in court in a few months!"

I was appalled. This was a mistake of vast proportion and I had failed my dearest friend and her father, both of whom I loved most desperately.

"I hope you had a good time off of work," Mr. Fisk said, handing Mrs. Miller a glass of cool lemonade.

"I did. It was a blast! And wouldn't you know my ex-husband paid for all of it." She knocked Fran with her pointed elbow, sending Fran's drink splattering on her clothing. "He'll find out when he gets his credit card bill."

I attempted to salvage any bit of honor that Mrs. Miller still held on to by steering the conversation into more pleasant territory. "And how is your piano playing going, Mrs. Miller? Do you have any upcoming concerts or venues where you will be performing?"

"Speaking of piano, you should've seen the look on my ex-husband's face when he came home from work and the piano was gone. It was priceless! See, I hid a camera behind a picture on the mantel and filmed the whole thing—"

"So," Mr. Fisk said, trying to salvage the conversation as well, "I should maybe call you in about a month to schedule the lessons?"

"Hmm," Mrs. Miller said, touching a hot-pink claw to her lips. "That should be fine. I have a hearing in a few weeks and, like I said, a few surgeries. But yep, call me in a month." She stood up.

Mr. Fisk stood as well, but I was too stunned in spirit and mind to bear any movement. "It seems like you're doing really well after your divorce," Mr. Fisk said, pulling a card from his wallet. "I had a rough time myself. Glad I had Cheryl Reiner—she's a counselor, you know—to help me through it."

Mrs. Miller stood, her face suddenly appearing sad and forlorn. "Really? Well, I'll think about it if I have a bad day or something." She extended her hand. "I actually can't stay long. My ex-husband works late tonight and I really want the toaster and a few other things. We'll do dessert another time." She started for the door, and though I mourned the loss of this opportunity to unite Mr. Fisk with his true love, I wished even more that dear Mrs. Miller would heal from her recent divorce—something her heart was obviously still crushed and broken by.

When the door was closed, Mr. Fisk turned and started for his office. "Well, that was easy. We'll call her in a month, though I think it might be a little longer. Healing takes time."

The door clicked closed, and I sunk into the couch in a mire of broken hopes and failed dreams. "That did not go well, I fear," I said. "But I am sure there is another woman—"

"Oh, no you don't, Polly Madassa! You said you'd stop," Fran said, plopping down next to me. "Remember how you promised? Besides, I think Ruthie is just the right girl for my dad, I just know it. And I know you'll like her once you meet her. Finally I'll have a mother around like you do!" She clapped her hands together and giggled. "In fact, she'll be here tomorrow! I can't wait."

Fran was indeed correct. I had vowed to stop matchmaking. Though I wished I had not, I was not a lady who would go back on her word. So I took my dearest friend's hand in mine. "Yes, I did. And I, Polly Madassa, will keep my solemn vow."

But as I rode home that summer's eve, the stars twinkling like bits of diamonds in the heavens, I realized that hope still remained.

Yes, I had promised to stop the search for Mr. Fisk's love, but I had made no promise that I would not attempt to protect Mr. Fisk and Fran from the unknown Miss Ruthie Carmichael.

I would be near to them when she arrived just one day hence, for I was still uncertain and skeptical of her character.

And in that way, I might still aid in saving my dearest friend and her father in the end.

Upon entering my home I remembered that Clementine's date of disaster with Clint was this very evening and was immediately agitated by the absence of her presence in the house. Her shoes were still missing and after making a careful and thorough search of her bedroom, I found she had not returned home for the evening.

Had Edward arrived on time? Had he rescued Clementine? Were they now gazing into each other's eyes with the first sparks of love igniting between them?

Thus with these thoughts, worry and extreme anxiety besought my spirit and I took refuge in my room, though peace of mind would not be mine that night. Not with the knowledge of Ruthie Carmichael arriving tomorrow and Clementine's current situation so precarious. In regards to my sister's happiness and joy, I was completely reliant upon Edward.

I took up a new book that I had not yet read, *Jane Eyre*, but could not concentrate under such duress of spirit and placed the leather-bound book back upon my bookshelf after a few moments.

And I must have fallen into a deep slumber, for all at once I was awoken by loud stomping coming up the stairs and the words, *"Where is she?"*

Had an intruder entered our home?

My heart thumped hard and I clutched at my chest as a figure, wild with rage, entered my room.

My dearest Clementine?

"Of all the evil things to do to a person!" She stomped into my bedroom, causing the hanging crystals adorning my antique lamp to clatter harshly against one another.

"What? What do you mean?" I asked, backing up against the headboard.

"Tonight, Clint, that Eddie guy . . . the whole thing, that's what!"

I could tell by my sister's wet hair and clothes, her scarlet cheeks, and the flames that seemed to dance in her eyes that things had not gone as I had planned with Edward. I had only beheld my sister this angered but once in my life, when I had borrowed her diary for nightly reading and had been remiss in returning it to her before she had found out. "I see that you are angry, my dear sister," I said, seeking to appease her.

"Do you realize what you did?"

Indeed, she was not to be appeased at this moment.

"You fell in love with Edward?" I asked, though all hope for that seemed to drain out of me with the look of extreme and terrifying anger she turned on me.

"No, Polly. I did not. There . . . there was the drink and the pizza, and then Edward throwing them into the ocean, then . . . then Clint bumping his head and getting knocked out, and then there were the jellyfish stings when we all fell into the water after Clint woke up and wrestled Edward right off the edge of the pier." Her voice had grown shaky and then panicked and then filled with wailing sobs as she described the scene that had occurred.

Indeed, I winced at the jellyfish stings lying in harsh slashes across her left leg.

"Oh my gosh!" Indeed, things had gone terribly wrong. "I . . . I'm sorry, Clemmy. I didn't mean for all that to happen. Really, I didn't. I guess, I messed up? I didn't think—"

"Messed up? Messed *up*? Oh, you messed up all right. You messed up my life, Polly. Ruined it!"

"But I didn't mean to mess it up. I was trying to help it! You were supposed to fall in love with Edward. And then Clint would be gone, you would be happy, and we'd be friends again, like we used to be." The words streamed like a fountain from my mouth.

"Edward? His name is Eddie, Polly. And no, I didn't fall in love with him and he is not in love with me. But you know what? Now Clint thinks that something really did happen between us and he has officially dumped me for good!" Tears sprang to her eyes and rolled down her cheeks.

"I'm sorry, Clemmy." I sat up and tried to soothe her by taking her hand in mine. I imagined what Elizabeth would say to her dear sister Jane. "I did it for your happiness alone." It did not work.

She jumped up and stomped toward the door. "My happiness? You mean yours! When did you decide that you should be in charge of other people's lives, Polly? What do you know about what makes me happy?!" She wagged her finger at me in a menacing way. "I will never, *never* speak to you again. *Ever!*"

And the door slammed shut behind her.

I fell back against my pillow, missing the goose-down feathers and ramming my head into the white headboard.

What had I done?

The fact that she would not fall deeply and truly in love with the gallant Edward had not occurred to me.

Mr. Darcy had rescued Elizabeth's family from ruin, and this had opened her eyes to the fact that she loved him.

And through this I had sought to rekindle the deep sisterly camaraderie between us.

But it hadn't worked. Rather it had only flung us further asunder.

I picked up the leather-bound copy of *Pride and Prejudice* and clutched it to my chest.

Where had I gone wrong?

Tears pooled in my eyes and overflowed down my cheeks at the thought of my beloved sister angry with me . . . even hating me.

And never speaking to me?

Surely she did not mean those words. Surely, upon the morrow, after the first shock of this had worn off, she would realize the good I had done.

But what if she didn't?

The tears came much faster.

First I failed Mr. Fisk and Fran, and now Clementine.

Was I cursed?

Was everything I touched doomed to dissolve love rather than ignite it into a burning flame?

In charge of people's lives? Could it be?

I stood upon weary legs and went to the window, kneeling by the full moon and folding my hands in earnest supplication. "I shall never interfere again," I vowed. And when the words had floated away on the breeze, I collapsed into a fit of tears that lasted until I fell into a restless sleep.

chapter twenty-one

In Which I Am Shunned, Ashamed, and Filled with Utter Despair

Clementine refused conversation the next morning, even though I sought to appease her with words of sincerest apology, pleas of forgiveness, and freshly baked pastries.

She was not to be moved. Instead, her ears and heart were sealed to my cries.

And no refuge could be found in Mama and Papa, who, I truly hoped, did not know of my unfortunate sin. To reveal it to them myself would bring a terrible wrath upon my head. Besides, if she had not already, I figured Clementine would tell them what I had done eventually.

And so the harbor I sought to ease my troubled soul was the romance of Miss Wiskerton and dear Mr. Nightquist. But the ride down the street bore me no joy, even though the sun beat down splendidly on my shoulders and the salty air seemed to carry me on a floating cloud down the sidewalk. Alas, I froze my heart to its comforts, for I had wounded my dearest sister more deeply than ever before and would now be a stranger to her.

I came to a halt at Miss Wiskerton's gate with eyes that were puffy with despair, and a throat burning with thick agony.

"If that's for me, I don't want it." I hadn't noticed Miss Wiskerton already lounging on her chair, *Pride and Prejudice* open on her lap.

"Pardon?" I asked, sure that my ears had deceived me.

"You heard me. If that's a pastry from Nightquist, I don't want it."

The small box trembled in my hands. This could not be! "But . . . but . . . Mr. Nightquist would want you to have it," I started, fearing that another attempt at holy matrimony had failed. "I thought that yesterday you were to lunch with him, Melissa Anne, and little Charles."

"Charles? Huh, I think his name should be Terror in Overalls, if you ask me! Did you hear what that little demon did to my poor Jack?"

"No, I . . ." I searched the yard for the nipping beast but found no trace of the little canine and his red collar. "Is he . . . ?"

"Dead? No, thank God. He's only slightly traumatized."

"Well, what happened?" I held out the pastry like a peace offering on Mr. Nightquist's behalf. "I find it hard to believe that my dear Mr. Nightquist would allow anything to harm a little creature, no matter how unlovable he may be. And I know that Charles has his faults but I cannot imagine it from him either. Really, this must all be—"

Miss Wiskerton leaned forward and placed her hands on her hips, posing a formidable figure. "Nightquist and Charlie took my dear Jack for a walk together. Like a fool, Nightquist handed Charlie the leash, and the little terror let go of it and my precious Jack scrambled into the street. He always loved to chase cars, you know. And well, he was hit."

"Hit by a car?" The image was very gruesome in my own imagination.

"Well, no. A bike rider. But he was going very fast."

I failed to see where Mr. Nightquist was at fault in all of this. "It doesn't sound like it was dear Mr.

Nightquist's fault, though," I said, attempting to ban the image of the motionless canine from my thoughts. "And though it was Charles's fault, he is but a boy, and surely you will forgive them both, especially since Jack is still breathing and alive. This unfortunate accident could easily happen to anyone."

"Not to me it couldn't! He was careless, and neither of them seemed to even like Jack. I suspect Nightquist had it planned from the start. The bone he brought over for him was probably a chicken bone meant to finish off my poor dog."

This I could not believe. I fought most heartily to keep Mr. Nightquist's name in good standing with the wounded woman and knew that if she would take the pastry I offered her, she would accept an apology from both Charles and Mr. Nightquist.

"Oh, but you can't really believe that, right? I don't believe it for an instant. Jack, as you know, is strong and bold, and I'm sure it was a mistake that has now blighted Mr. Nightquist's heart forever. And the remorse that Charles feels is most likely a burden no child should be made to bear... even if he is obstinate and out of control."

She reached for the bag and I relinquished it in hope that this meant that her heart was softening once more. "You really think he's upset about the whole thing?"

"Oh, I would not be surprised if he lay upon his bed, unwilling to arise unless he knows his mistake has been forgiven."

"Hmmm, I hope he is sorry," she said while biting into the chocolate croissant. "But, I'd hate to see him too torn up about it. The vet did say that Jack just needed a little time off his feet. Maybe if you see him today you can tell him that I don't wish he was dead and that he can stop by for a bit if he wants."

I placed my hands over my heart. "Upon my word, good lady, I will visit him upon completion of my other deliveries. Surely your words will be like water to a parched and thirsty soul, Miss Wiskerton. Now please, give my good wishes to Jack as he mends. Good day." And I set off down the sidewalk.

Was there no hope? Sorrow filled me up to the brim, and hot tears fell down my face. Surely, I had ruined any chance of love for dear Mr. Nightquist, and Clementine had renounced me as her sister. And I had even failed my bosom friend Fran, and who knows what the woman Ruthie Carmichael was really like? Maybe she was a raging lunatic and because of my failure my dearest friends would be lost forever.

"Hopeless," I said aloud. "Hopeless, hopeless, hopeless."

Yet hadn't Miss Wiskerton given me a tiny reason to believe that perhaps she would forgive Mr. Nightquist and his wretched grandson?

My heart dared to beat with promise again, and I replayed her final words over and over in my mind. "You can tell him that I do not wish him to plunge into the grave," she had said. "But you may tell him that if he so wishes to continue to court me, he can come calling on me today and I will wait for him in earnest." And if those weren't her exact words, they were quite similar, I was sure. I allowed a very small smile to grace my face as I journeyed home, plans to meet him later on this afternoon forming in my mind.

Maybe, just maybe, I could still salvage one romance.

After completing my deliveries, I made another attempt at appeasing Clementine's fury by writing a letter of extreme apology in my most delicate calligraphy hand. I slipped it under her closed door in hopes that within minutes our bond as sisters would once again be restored.

I was sorely mistaken.

The letter came back in a million pieces and once more my heart was dashed against the rocks of her unyielding fury.

I cradled the torn pieces in my hand and cried. "Clemmy, I'm sorry," I lamented through the door. "Really, I... I was just trying to... help you. I thought you'd... you'd like Eddie. Please, don't be mad at me for keeps. Please!"

"Polly, I will never forgive you!" she yelled.

At her harsh words, I couldn't help but sit down in the hall and cry. And once I began, I could not stop, for my heart ached inside me over what I'd done, and over what I'd lost.

I hoped that as I lamented she would be softened toward me, would come to the door and forgive me, but her heart was like stone, which only served to make the tears come harder and faster.

I needed to talk with someone.

Someone who would try to understand and comfort me or tell me what I should do. I retreated to my room, where I tried telephoning Fran, but my calls went unanswered. So I went to seek out Mr. Nightquist. In part to bandage the wound between him and Miss Wiskerton, and in part in need of his consolation in my hour of desperate need.

I found him at his kite shop, a look of despair upon his face. Charles, the little beast, seemed not as remorseful as he darted in between the aisles of the shop, paying no heed to the items that fell in his wake. Melissa Anne was nowhere to be seen, but a tuna casserole sat upon the counter—another blight to Mr. Nightquist's soul.

"Hi, Mr. Nightquist," I called out.

He gazed up at me and smiled. "Oh hello, Polly girl. How are you today?"

"Much troubled in spirit, I'm afraid." I sat upon a stool, my chin resting in my hands. "I have heard of the unfortunate accident with Jack and your grandson."

He shook his head. "I guess I knew I shouldn't have given Charlie the leash, but I wanted him to like Eugenia May, and he's always wanted a dog of his own. And then it all happened faster than I could stop it. Then Eugenia was crying, Charlie was screaming, and Missy was trying to calm them both down while I got the vet." He ran his ruddy hands through his hair. "That's that. And now I'm realizing how much I was starting to like her. But it's over and I gotta remind myself of that."

He said these words with such heart-wrenching

finality that fresh tears pricked at my eyes. Yet I knew hope remained. "But dear Mr. Nightquist, I have just come from her home. And though she is still much upset, she now realizes that the fault could have been upon anyone. I'm sure if you and dear Charles would offer an apology, she would open her heart to you."

"You think?" Mr. Nightquist's eyes were filled with hope once more. "That's what she said?"

"Indeed it is, my dear sir. You must go to her and make amends, and then all will be right between you."

He slapped the counter and laughed. "Well, all right then. Me and Charlie will head on down there right after lunch! What do you say, Charlie?"

At this Charles let out a very loud, "No, I don't wanna," which made me doubt the course that Mr. Nightquist was on.

But Mr. Nightquist was filled with excitement and paid no heed to the rebellious lad. Instead, he hugged me around my dainty shoulder. "Thanks, Polly!"

And though I longed to unburden my own soul to this kindred spirit, I could not when he was so filled with happiness and love's calling.

So instead I bid him good luck and went on my way.

By evening, I was in desperate need of comforting from my bosom friend. Surely Fran and her father would console my heavy heart!

But alas, when I telephoned dear Fran, there was no answer.

Once more, yet still no answer.

Then it became all too clear.

The woman, Miss Ruthie Carmichael, had arrived this very day. My mind, plagued with disconcerting thoughts of Clementine, had let this information slip away until now.

But why, then, did Fran not answer my telephone calls? Surely she wanted me with her to share in her joy and to approve of her father's choice?

Or had Miss Carmichael arrived and immediately put Fran and Mr. Fisk to death? Or were my dearest friends held hostages in their own home, awaiting only the arrival of a kindred spirit willing to come to their aid? What if she had bewitched Mr. Fisk into running away with her, and dearest Fran was now a prisoner in an orphanage forced to make lace doilies and eat gruel?!

My heart pulsed hard in my chest as I thought of

their agonizing plight. Together, barricaded in the basement by the evil Miss Carmichael, they lamented to one another, "Why, oh why did we not listen to Polly? She would've found someone wonderful, but alas, we paid no heed. Now who will save us?"

"I will save you," I said aloud, determined that I must make my way to their home at once.

And if not save them . . . perish with them.

The golden clock, now back on my nightstand, struck the tenth hour as I hurried to leave. Mama and Papa had long since gone to bed and my estranged sister was still in her room, as she had remained throughout the day.

So, in silence, I slipped off my bed and into the cornflower-blue dress with the elegant waist. I went to the window and breathed deeply of the salty air and heard the ocean calling me to "go, go, go." And, so that I did not wake my father and mother from slumber nor disturb my sister's silent laments, I tiptoed down the stairs and out the back doorway.

I rode to Fran's home straightaway, fear for my dearest friend pushing me forward, yet the sadness over Clementine weighing my heart down like dampened sand.

Yet my fears only intensified as I rounded the corner and heard the screams and squeals coming from their home.

If only they had heeded my warnings.

I dropped my bike to the ground with a terrorizing clang as metal hit concrete, and stopped at the edge of their lawn. Through the window, a strange woman (surely it was Ruthie Carmichael) laughed, a wicked smile upon her lips.

Surely not! My whole body was consumed in fright, but though I felt I might fall into a swoon, I kept myself upright.

Had all my fears come true?

I looked harder at the scene and saw no one but the infamous Ruthie Carmichael. She lifted up her hand as if to stab someone and I covered my eyes, letting out an ear-piercing scream over the horror of it all. I could not witness my bosom friend and her father succumbing to such an end.

But I had to do something. The Internet woman really and truly was a malicious killer.

"What in the name of all that's holy is going on out here?" a voice called from next door. "Who's screaming out here?"

I ignored the voice at first and ran up to the Fisks' front window.

Fran was nowhere to be seen. Could it be that her life had already ended?

The woman, both beautiful and deadly, laughed heartily with her hands clutched around the neck of Mr. Fisk. His tongue hung out of his mouth grotesquely and he looked on the verge of certain death.

Words caught in my throat, and I let out another scream, louder than the first. This startled Ruthie and she jumped, most likely aware that she had been caught in the act of such vile deeds.

"What's going on?!" the voice next door called out again. "If you don't tell me who you are and what you're doing over there I'll call the police!"

Yes! That was what needed to be done. I ran toward the voice and saw it was Mrs. Fowler, Fran and Mr. Fisk's next-door neighbor. "Please! Please! Help me! Quick! We need to call the police."

Mrs. Fowler grabbed at my arm. "Polly? Is that you? What's wrong? Why are you screaming?"

"It's Fran and Mr. Fisk!" I said, panting. "There's a woman, an evil woman, in their house. Just look! Her name is Ruthie Carmichael." I dragged the fearful lady onto the Fisks' front lawn and pointed into the window, where Miss Carmichael had resumed strangling poor Mr. Fisk, her face twisted into a laughing smile. "Mr. Fisk met her on the Internet and thought she was in love with him. Little did he know that her only intention was to end his life!"

Again, my body felt so overwhelmed with fear that I thought I might fall to the ground in a faint. But I stood fast, knowing that I must be ready to aid my friend when the authorities arrived. Perhaps I could nurse her back to health or my own blood could help save her if she needed a transfusion.

"Are you sure?" the woman asked.

"Of course I'm sure, just look at her!"

"All right, I'll be back," she said, and left me alone in the yard, tears streaming down my cheeks.

But I couldn't look at the scene. Instead I wailed and cried, counting the minutes, the seconds, before the sound of the sirens could be heard.

A policeman arrived moments later, lights flashing blue and red in the dark, dark night. They surrounded the house at once, and I watched in horror as Fran, who I had not seen earlier, fell to the ground in a heap while Ruthie Carmichael took a bow. She had finished them both off.

"Oh, Fran!" I yelled.

"Ruthie Carmichael!" the police shouted through his bullhorn. "Come out with your hands above your head."

I spied Ruthie Carmichael at the window glancing into the streets. Then, thankfully, Mr. Fisk arose and looked out as well, though I feared for his close proximity to Miss Carmichael. Fran got up next and I heaved a sob of relief at the sight of her alive and well. Their will to live had overcome death.

All three of them exited the house. "What is all this?" Mr. Fisk asked.

"Down!" the policeman said. "We need Miss Carmichael down on the ground."

Ruthie Carmichael lowered herself to the ground. "What's going on? What did I do?"

And then there was a great commotion like I had never seen before as Miss Carmichael was hauled away for questioning by the police and Mr. Fisk chased after the authorities, assuring them "everything was fine" and that it was all "just a game."

Fran found me and I grasped her hands in mine and kissed them. "Oh, my dearest friend. I am so relieved that you are unhurt! When I saw that woman's hands upon your father's neck, I was sure you were killed—"

She tore her hands from mine, her eyes flashing with fury and rage that I'd only seen once when her young cousin broke her favorite china doll. But that was when she was but a child of seven. "*You did this?* How... how could you, Polly?" Her chin trembled and she backed away. "I should've known you'd come and ruin all this."

"Huh? I... I saw her trying to kill your dad.... I was only trying to... to save you."

"Save me?" she yelled into the now-still night. Tears streamed down her cheeks. "We were playing a game! And I don't need you to save me! I don't need you to help me, Polly! It's like you're trying to take away any chance of happiness I have. It's like you want me to be sad and without a mom!"

Tears now poured from my own eyes. "That's not true, Fran. You know it's not. You have to. I just thought—"

"You didn't think, Polly! This isn't your dumb Green Gables or England or whatever. This is real life. This is *my* life and you're ruining it! You have no idea what it's been like to not have my mom. To see my dad sad all the time. Now, we have a chance to maybe be happy, and you step in and chase any hope of that away. Just leave!" And into the black night she fled.

"But Fran!" I yelled. "I'm sorry!"

She whirled back around. "Just go away!"

Hot tears ran down my face, scourging my heart. Indeed, I deserved her hate, and her rage, and all of her malicious thoughts. So, without picking up my bicycle, I dashed home, unable to enjoy the wind blowing through my rustling dress or the stars that sparkled like diamonds in the deep black sky.

Instead, sorrow and despair were my companions.

When I reached my humble home, I did not enter. I did not wish to defile my house, so ashamed I was of yet another grave mistake. Instead, I lay down underneath the delicate branches of the maple tree. And though I had always thought it romantic to sleep under the shade of this proud tree, the damp, sparse grass itched my skin, and the feeling of loneliness and despair lay on top of me like a blanket. The tears I wept watered the ground beneath me.

Neither the words of *Anne of Green Gables* nor the assurance of enduring love found in *Pride and Prejudice* could offer consolation or comfort now. How could they?

"I'm hopeless," I cried aloud. "I've ruined everyone

and everything. And now, I've lost my sister and my best friend!"

And I cried like I'd never done before, until somewhere in a fit of exhaustion I fell into a restless and painful sleep.

chapter twenty-two

In Which I Am Shunned Once More

Things did not improve upon break of day. And though *Anne of Green Gables* had stated that tomorrow is always fresh with no mistakes in it, I awoke with the mistakes of my recent past hovering over my head like a black shroud of death.

"Polly? Polly?" It was Papa's voice. I gazed upon him and beheld his surprised countenance. "What are you doing out here? You didn't sleep under the tree all night, did you?"

I sat up and nodded, my neck and back aching with the aftereffects of a night on the ground and my heart filled up to the brim with sorrow. I sighed and allowed myself to be lifted to my feet, though the heaviness in my heart was still very much there.

"Are you all right, Polly?" he asked. Mama had

joined him at his side, and she hugged me to her.

I sobbed into her shoulder, and she led me into the house and sat with me upon the couch.

"Now, tell me what this is all about."

"My life, my life is a perfect graveyard of buried hopes," I lamented. I had read that in *Anne of Green Gables*, and though I had longed to use it, I never imagined a moment so terrible I'd be able to speak those words.

"Oh, come on. Nothing is that bad. Did you and Fran have a fight?"

I nodded, tears cascading down my cheeks.

"So, what happened?"

"I got her potential mother arrested and ruined any chance at her having happiness."

Mama sat up straight. "Arrested? Who did you have arrested?"

"The lady who Mr. Fisk met on the computer."

"Oh my gosh, Polly. How did this happen?"

I recounted the story through tears that shook my shoulders and brought the fresh pain of what I had done to the surface once more.

Mama shook her head. "How could you do that, Polly?"

Now that the floodgate of sins was open, I released everything I had done all at once. "But that's not the end of it all. I broke up Clementine and Clint. First I wrote them each a letter saying that they were breaking up with the other. But when that didn't work, I had Edward, this boy at the toy store, try to rescue Clementine from Clint. I thought that Edward and Clementine would fall in love but they didn't, and now Clementine has jellyfish stings and hates me, and Fran hates me. And I'm sure Mr. Nightquist will hate me too."

"Mr. Nightquist? Why would *he* hate you?"

"Because I set him up with Miss Wiskerton and then he let Jack get hit by a bike and now Miss Wiskerton hates him. And then there was Lucy Penny."

"Wait, wait, wait. What in the world have you been doing?"

I wiped my tears with the back of my hand and blew my nose into my dress, something that in any other circumstance I would never, ever consider doing. "I've been trying to help people . . . fall in love."

All was silent, except for my quiet sobbing. Finally Mama spoke. "It seems you've been letting your romanticism get the best of you again." She stood up and paced the floor. "I thought there had to be a reason why Clementine has been so upset. She said Clint and her are over . . . through."

"I am afraid what you say is true. At my hands they have been pulled asunder."

Papa sat upon the couch and placed his arm around me. "Breaking up people is a dangerous thing, Polly. You know, your mother and I almost didn't get married."

The words stunned me and I sat up straight, wondering at his meaning. That could not be!

Mama smiled. "Your dad's grandma didn't like me at all. What'd she say about me, Sam?"

Papa smiled. "Oh, I don't even remember anymore. But I do remember she was always trying to break us up. She liked this girl named Sally Seawald and hoped I'd date and marry her. Ha!"

Mama smiled as well, though I was mortified at the thought. My great-grandmother was just like Lady Catherine de Bourgh in the great *Pride and Prejudice*—trying to tear asunder those who were meant to be together. To think that neither Clementine nor I would be here on the earth was something I could not bear. Or perhaps my name would have been

Grenhilda—a name that I had decided was the worst name a person could be called.

A terrible fate.

"She told him one time that I was dating some other guy, 'cause she saw me hugging my cousin," Mama said, walking over to Papa and grasping his hand in her own.

"I broke up with her, and we didn't see each other for almost a full year after that."

"But then the two of you met once more upon the shores of love," I said, knowing this romantic part of the story.

Papa laughed. "Well, it wasn't all 'shores of love' at first, but we made it through, and that's all that mattered."

Mama stepped in. "So just think, if we hadn't met each other on the beach that day, who knows if we would ever have seen each other again? You don't mess with people's lives, Polly. You can't."

A fresh wave of weeping swept over me. "I'm . . . I'm sorry. I need to go upstairs," I declared through heart-wrenching sobs.

And once in my room, I threw myself upon the bed and wailed at the great sin I had committed against my sister. To interrupt love's working was the greatest sin; I had declared it to my own soul more than once.

Yet it was I . . . I who had betrayed love.

And I had betrayed my dearest sister. And though I highly doubted that Clint could ever become gentlemanly or exciting, or that he and Clementine were meant for each other, I supposed there was always the slim (and indeed, I believed it was slim) possibility.

I did not wish to become like the high-and-mighty Lady Catherine, who had found it her duty to save her nephew from his one true love.

The thought, the painful thought of this made my heart wrench and twist inside my chest.

But even more painful was the chasm I had set between my own dear sister and myself.

My fate was surely to stay locked inside my bedroom like a prisoner, for what comfort should a thwarter of love receive? I would never come out. Instead I would live, a hermit, away from those I had wounded so deeply. Surely the very sight of me would only bring pain to their hearts.

The tears poured from my eyes, and I wallowed in despair. All that I had hoped and dreamed for concerning those I loved had failed disastrously. I was in a prison of buried hopes.

I clutched *Anne of Green Gables* in my hands and beseeched the spirit of her to aid me in this time. "Dearest Anne, my kindred spirit. What must I do to heal those I have hurt?" And with eyes tight shut, I waited for an answer, a bit of advice that would assist me on this journey of redeeming myself, if in fact I could be redeemed.

But no answer did come.

No aid.

No assistance.

I was alone with my tormented and troubled soul.

And I thought of my dear Clementine, realizing that she, too, was most troubled.

All because of me.

That was it. I must try to persuade her to forgive me. I knew that her heart was far from me, and that although she had not heard my former pleas of redemption, I must continue to try. I must not stop in this quest.

I could not.

But how?

She would not hear words, nor would she listen to the language of pastries. No, her heart was closed to me.

I needed to prove that I was filled with deep regret over my treacherous sin.

And there was but one way, I knew.

I must attempt at bringing Clint and my dear sister back together. The words, indeed, were very hard to say. But it was true.

It was I who tore them apart, and it must be I who brought them back together.

After composing myself, I raced down the stairway in search of my sister to tell her of my plan.

Surely her heart would soften.

"Clementine? Clementine, can I talk to you for just a second?" I called. But no answer came.

"She's not here, Polly," Mama called from the kitchen. "I think she went out on the beach for a walk."

Perhaps she and Clint would meet just like Mama and Papa did! Indeed, I needed to be present for this moment. To tell them how deeply sorry I was and to bless their relationship. I placed my hat atop my head and walked out the door and straight into Bradley's waiting figure.

"Oh my gosh, Brad!" I cried out in alarm. "Um... surely you frightened me beyond reason. Why have you come?"

Upon his head he wore an elegant black top hat. He was clothed in a somewhat overly large black coat and held a cane in one hand and a single stem of lily of the valley in the other. His cheeks filled with color that agreed with his appearance, and though I felt myself drawn to his person, I refused.

A wretched killer of romance and love did not deserve love in return!

"Well, I... I heard about what happened with Fran and her dad last night."

"What?! How in the world do you know?" With my many sins, I had forgotten, momentarily, what I had done to my bosom friend.

Did my wretchedness know no bounds?

He looked down at the sidewalk. "Well, my mom's a cop. She was working last night and was the one that helped sort everything out at the station."

Now it was my cheeks that filled with deep red, and I could not stop the tears from coming. "I didn't mean to ruin everything," I said. "It's just that I wanted her to have a mom again—the perfect mom. And finding someone on the Internet, it's just not... not... not right." I sat down upon the sidewalk and concealed my face with my hands, hoping he would not look upon me.

He sat beside me, but spoke not a word.

"Tell me, Brad. Did your mom say if everything is all right? Or is she in jail?"

"No, she's not in jail. Actually, she was laughing about it in the end, my mom said. But . . . I did see Fran today."

My heart pounded hard within my chest. "What . . . I mean . . . did she say anything about me or about what happened?" I wished with all of my heart that perhaps she had forgiven me already, and had even laughed over the matter herself.

"Well, she said that you never listen to her, that you have no idea how hard it's been for her without a mom, and that . . . that she never wants to see you again."

A torrent of sadness and tears overcame me at hearing this. My heart was crushed and would never rise up again, I was sure. And though Brad was not my confidante, I couldn't help the words that poured out of me. "Oh, Brad! What should I do? I thought I always listened to her, and I know it's been hard for her not to have a mom. She's my bosom friend, and I can't live without my bosom friend."

He sighed. "I don't know about bosom friends or girl stuff or anything like that. But you know when my dad left it was real hard." He did not look up but twisted his hands. I knew at once that this was hard for him to say, and he did so to help me.

"All of a sudden I was the man of the house. My mom had to go back to working full-time, I was home by myself a lot, and I had to learn how to cook and clean. Then there was the school stuff and sports and things. The father-son basketball game, the father-son football game. And I didn't get to go to any of it, 'cause I didn't have a dad of my own." He shook his head. "I know my mom could've gone, but that would've been even worse, besides the fact she was always working."

I did not speak, for I had nothing to say in response.

"When he left it changed everything, Pol... Polly. And you know what I wanted most?"

"Someone to aid you through the time of trial? Someone that would lend you their father like I lent out my mother to Fran?"

His laughter at this surprised me. "No, Polly. It would've been nice just to have someone listen to me and try to understand where I was coming from."

He stood up at this moment. "I actually came over to ask you if you wanted to go for a really cool... I mean, elegant dinner on the board of the walk." He took off his hat. "But maybe another time, huh?"

I nodded, but gave him a small smile before he walked away.

And seeing his retreating figure depart, I was no longer filled with any hope of reconciliation with my bosom friend, nor with my sister.

All that Fran had wanted from me was a listening ear and a kindred heart of understanding. But I had given her neither.

And at these terrible thoughts, anguish and hopelessness filled me up so fully and completely that I felt I would break in two. I covered my face with my hands. "What have I done?"

I turned back to my house, and could hardly stand to look up at the window of my room where I had concocted my villainous plans. "What have I done?" I cried again. Unable to go inside, I ran down to the beach to try and sort through all that had happened at my own hand. Surely, I could find some solace in the waves, some sort of plan of redemption.

Besides, with all those I loved angry with me, where else was there to go?

chapter twenty-three

In Which I Fall into the Sea and Am Plagued with Scarlet Fever, Consumption, or Some Other Rare and Deadly Disease

I walked along the shore, letting the water lap at my ankles and drench the hem of my dress. Fresh tears sprung from my eyes and a new torment filled my heart.

I was cursed, and lifelong sorrow was all I was destined for now.

"Ouch!" My toe hit a slick, sharpened rock, and I realized I had come upon the jetty that reached out into the ocean's breaking waves. Most did not venture out onto the jagged pier, but I had navigated the rocks long ago with my parents by my side and then with Fran accompanying me.

I started along its weatherworn path.

The wind pummeled me and the water spray smote my face with angry lashes. It was what I deserved, and though the pain brought fresh tears to my eyes, I bore it all for the pain that I had exacted on those whom I loved.

My feet ached beneath me as a rock seemed to reach out and pierce my flesh. The cold, salted ocean stung the freshly opened skin and I winced. But farther I ventured, out past the breakers until the jetty ended and the open, wild sea began.

I stared below me at the waves crashing together in a surge of angry water. What had I done? I was now beginning to realize the full extent, and it was more than I could bear.

"Polly?"

I opened my eyes as the waves spoke my name. Could it be the spirit of the sea calling to me from its watery depths? Having so angered the ways of love, was I now causing this squall upon the sea?

"Polly?" Again the voice spoke.

The sound was not coming from below me but from behind me.

I turned to see Mr. Nightquist, a kite in hand, walking toward me, his arms beckoning me to turn back. "Polly? For all that's holy," he screamed above the din of the ocean. "What are you doing out here?"

"I was . . . I was just—" But as I stepped toward his open palm, my wounded foot slipped and I fell into the surging water below.

I swam through a sea of melting visions. A black top hat, a kite, kind eyes, silver braces.

Finally, I heard a voice. "Polly? Polly?"

"Come on." I felt a tapping on my arm and my head being lifted up. "Come on, wake up."

"What's going on? Where am I?" I mumbled. My eyes flickered open and beheld a haze of light and the silhouette of a head and shoulders. After blinking again and again, the vision clarified, and I awoke in the kite shop with Bradley above me. My heart thumped wildly in my chest at the sight of him.

My hero. Indeed he had saved me.

"Oh good, you're awake." Mr. Nightquist came to my side and held my hand in his own.

"What happened?" I asked, my mouth dry and my throat aching. I attempted to sit but was pierced by a fierce ache in my head that kept me reclined.

Mr. Nightquist leaned back against the cabinet and sighed. "Girl, you gave me and this young guy quite a scare. You slipped right off the end of that jetty."

I gazed upon Bradley, my knight in shining armor.

"Glad you're okay," he said, his face turning a handsome and bashful crimson.

But then the unpleasant memories of my misdeeds coursed through my veins. I rolled over, ashamed, wishing they had not saved such a wretched soul as I. Wishing that I had perished in the watery sea without having to face my sins. Becoming a sea wraith, mourning my sins in the ocean depths. "I can't go back. I'm so ashamed."

"Enough of that talk, Polly girl," Mr. Nightquist said, his rough hand upon mine.

The anguish returned like a tidal wave upon my soul. "Oh, but you don't know what I have done. Ruined lives lie in a wake behind me and I am hopeless."

"Hmmm," was all Mr. Nightquist said before he got up and left the room. Bradley followed behind. I had most likely ruined his and Miss Wiskerton's lives as well and should be banished from the sight of all mankind.

But dear Mr. Nightquist did not abandon me completely, for just as I had made up my mind to leave the shop and become a nomad roaming the earth like a plagued ghost, he emerged from the back and held out a steaming cup. "Here, it'll warm you up. Your parents should be here soon. I called them a few minutes ago. They were pretty worried." He stopped and gazed at me, one bushy eyebrow raised in suspicion. "Everything all right?"

And that is when I divulged all the wrong I had committed and the pain I had caused. "But I didn't mean for it to all go wrong, really. I just wanted things to work out like it did for Elizabeth and Mr. Darcy and Anne and Gil. You know, true love and happy ever after." I sniffed most inelegantly. "But instead I ruined everyone and everything. Clint and Clemmy are through, Clemmy hates my guts, and I'll be lucky if Fran ever speaks to me again."

I lowered my head in shame.

He spoke nothing at first but took the mug from my hand and smiled. "Hmm. Aren't Elizabeth and Darcy and the other names just characters in a book?"

"Why, yes," I said. "They enjoyed love's complete fullness in each other's arms."

He rubbed at his chin. "They did, did they? Well, did those people go through a divorce before they met?"

"No, certainly not."

"Did they lose their wives to death? Were they

teenagers in high school trying to figure out what love is? Had either of their parents been divorced before? Were they older men or women who'd never had a shot at love before?"

"I don't know," I said, quite confused at his questioning. "I'm not sure what you mean, Mr. Nightquist."

He stood to open the back door where a frantic knocking had commenced. "Well, Polly girl. I don't doubt that you wanted the best for us all. But love's not a book, is it?"

I did not understand, nor was my mind working properly to attempt to discover the mystery of his words, for both Papa and Mama entered the room and took me into their embrace. This only made the sting of my sins harsher inside me. The short drive home was silent and calm, and I began to feel feverish and dizzy, chills running up and down my spine. I welcomed the fever, if only to pay for my wrongdoing.

"You don't look too good, Polly," Mama said, placing the side of her soft cheek against my forehead. "I think you need to go upstairs and rest."

I trudged up to my room, the weight of the wet dress feeling light compared to the heaviness in my own heart.

I slipped into another gown and curled up under the covers, beckoning to the scarlet fever—for that is what I was certain I had succumbed to—that would give me my due.

And indeed, the fever did its work, and I spent the next few days in and out of sleep, shivering, dreaming, and drinking the warm chicken broth my mother held up to my lips. Dreams fluttered in and out in my mind and gave me no comfort, for they seemed only to taunt me with images of what I had done.

Yet it was what I deserved.

But late in the night of that third day I awoke into the darkness of my room sadly rejuvenated. I had been forced back into the land of the living with my transgressions still before me.

With the matches that I had secreted under my mattress many months before, I lit the candlestick in its candelabra and brought it to the nightstand. Writing by candlelight was utterly romantic, and after spending lifeless days in my bedroom, I needed its healing glow upon my heart and mind.

I needed its aid in helping me redeem myself.

Mr. Nightquist's words were called forth in my mind. "Love's not a book, is it?"

From the drawer beside my bed, I took out my stationery, calligraphy pen, and inkwell. I let the pen scratch across the surface of the paper.

I indeed wished for the happiness of those who were dearest to my heart.

But instead:

My dearest Clementine had lost the one she loved. This was because of me. I had wanted for her a man that I found suitable. But perhaps, to her (however far-fetched it seemed), Clint was Mr. Darcy.

My dearest Fran, my bosom friend, had most likely lost a potential mother, and Mr. Fisk a wife, who, though she was contacted through the Internet, was a good woman. This also was because of me. Although I felt like Mr. Fisk should be with someone more out of a novel, maybe for Mr. Fisk, Ruthie was as elegant and refined as Elizabeth.

I thought upon Bradley's honest words and Fran's spoken anger the night of my crime.

The two were correct. I hadn't listened to her. I hadn't truly understood or tried to understand what agony she must have endured over these years since her mother's departure. Instead, I had treated her feelings and her life like that of a character in a book. Something I could remedy and make right.

Mr. Nightquist's words struck to the quick of my soul.

I, Polly Madassa, thought myself and my own way the best for others and sought to force love rather than let love write its own story, no matter how unromantic to me it might have seemed.

Yes, this was truth.

And though I was utterly relieved to have uncovered just where I had taken a wrong path, the immensity of my mistakes was not erased or mended.

That would take ardent apologies and beseeching for forgiveness on my part. And so, with pen in hand, and alongside a heart filled with both heavy sadness and floating hope, I constructed a plan of redemption, which I would carry out that next day.

Whether or not my sins would be forgiven, I knew that I must confess my wrongdoings to those whom I had wounded so deeply.

chapter twenty-four

In Which I Seek to Make Amends with My Dearest Sister

I awoke the next morning with the beams of sunlight kissing my tear-stained face. The smells from below me were warm and fragrant, and I dwelt on their welcoming scent as I slipped into the shower and prepared myself for the task at hand.

I would confess first to Clementine, and attempt to restore our sisterly bond, if indeed it could be restored.

My heart pounded inside my chest as I descended the stairs in search of her. Twice, I was certain I was going to fall into a swoon, but was held up by the seriousness of my task.

I heard her quiet giggle coming from the kitchen and Mama's laughter as well, yet when I entered, both ceased.

Mama walked toward me, bestowing a kiss upon my alabaster forehead. "I'm glad you're feeling better, my Polly." And she left me alone with my sister—now a stranger to me.

Clementine was mixing a batch of something that smelled of cinnamon, and I went and stood beside her.

Truly, I could not stop the tears from coming. "I'm . . . I'm sorry, Clemmy," I managed between sobs. "I only wanted to make you happy and for us to be friends again. We used to have so much fun and now we don't. And I just wanted that back. But . . . but I was wrong to do what I did." I wiped my nose with a towel I found upon the counter. She did not respond, so I sniffed and composed myself. "And even though I do not think that Clint is the man for such a wonderful woman as yourself, I am prepared to go and seek him out on your behalf. I will tell him that it was all my fault and see if he will come over to see you. Give me the word and consider it done."

It was at these words that Clementine turned toward me. I shrunk away from her gaze, knowing that indeed the words to come might not be ones that I wanted to hear.

"I still can't believe you did that, Pol. I mean . . . that was like the lowest thing you could ever do."

Tears pricked at my eyes again. "I know, Clemmy. I'm sorry."

She sighed. "Well, at least you know what you did, and you won't do it again, ever!"

I nodded. "Would you like me to approach Clint and try to remedy the situation?"

She waved her hand. "No. We're officially done, and I'm all right. Besides, I met this guy on the beach yesterday who's really cute."

"Indeed?"

She turned and rolled her eyes at me. "Yes, his name is Sean, and he's coming into the shop in just a bit."

"Are you sure he is—?"

She pointed her finger at me. "Don't push it, Pol. And if you ever mess with my life again, I'll kill you."

"I vow that I will not, my dear Clementine. You have my solid vow."

And then my sister began to laugh quite loud, and quite indecently, she filled her hand with flour and threw it directly in my face. "Oh, shut it, Polly."

I was quite stunned at first, and could find no words.

"Oh, come, dearest," she said in a mocking voice.

"Surely thou hast a sense of humor. Dost thou?"

And though it was nice to hear her speak so delicately, I couldn't help but laugh as well. And after I had tossed my own handful of flour at her face, we had quite a fight until I fell through the doors into the bakery just in time to see a rather disheveled young man enter the bakery and look about. "Yo, is Clementine around?"

"Surely it cannot be," I said, but was whisked away by my mother into the kitchen, where Clementine was laughing hardily and dusting herself off.

"There's a boy here to meet you, Clemmy," Mama said, pinching my arm quite hard.

"Ouch, Mama!" I cried out. "My dear sister, you are quite a mess, I'm afraid. Though I guess you will match his . . . crumpled appearance."

"Shoot!" And she dashed for the hallway bathroom and came out looking decidedly better, though still quite covered with flour on her clothing.

"Are you sure you know what you are about, Clementine? I have seen him and am not afraid to survey this young man further for you," I said with full sincerity, though knowing I would not overstep my boundaries again.

She turned to me and wagged her finger. "Don't even

start, Pol." And she disappeared through the door.

I pressed my ear to the wood and listened.

"Hey, dude," the voice shouted at Clementine. "You look smokin' hot!"

And at these words I pulled my ear away. Surely hearing any further would only be temptation for me to stop this before it started. And I could not.

"I commit your life to love, dearest sister. No matter where it may lead." And at that I departed my home.

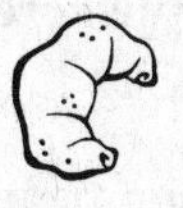

chapter twenty-five

In Which I Seek to Make Amends with My Bosom Friend and Her Father

It had been but days since I had last seen my bosom friend, yet it felt like years had come and gone between us.

And though my heart was relieved at Clementine's acceptance of my apology, I knew not what the next hours would bring, and that was a sobering thought indeed.

I strolled down the sidewalk, silently beseeching love to bring me courage and guidance in this time of trial to my soul. So intent upon my own thoughts was I that I did not notice the house of Miss Wiskerton until that genteel woman called out to me.

"Polly! Where are you headed?"

I turned to the woman and walked down her pathway lined with flowers. "Only seeking to make amends, my dear Miss Wiskerton. And to you, I must apologize as well."

Her hand went to her heart. "What in the world have you done, Polly Madassa? The neighborhood isn't on fire, is it?" she asked.

But I did not get a chance to reply, for at that moment Mr. Nightquist emerged from Miss Wiskerton's home with a plate of cookies, Charles following behind, and Jack the Nipper barking vengefully at their heels. "Oh, she hasn't done anything, Eugenia. At least not to us." And he winked at me upon setting the tray on a small glass table.

"Well, let's hope not," Miss Wiskerton declared, and picked up a cookie from the plate. "Now, Charlie, will you run in and get my sun hat?"

Charles, who had not seemed to have mended all of his ways, yelled out a rather loud and obstinate, "No!" and stuffed his mouth with at least three cookies.

Miss Wiskerton wagged a sausage finger at him. "You'll do as I say, Charlie, or you'll find yourself without supper tonight."

I watched the scene, quite astounded when Charles obeyed.

Mr. Nightquist and I exchanged knowing glances, and I suspected that dear Miss Wiskerton was a woman who could hold her own against the terror of a boy. And even more surprised was I when Charles came back with the bonnet and then hugged her.

Indeed, she was just what he and Mr. Nightquist needed.

"You wanna cookie, Polly?" Miss Wiskerton offered.

I sighed. "I will have to decline. My soul is tremulous at what I must do now, and I am afraid if I partake of food, I will indeed become quite sick."

"Well, maybe you could stop by tomorrow and we could talk about *Pride and Prejudice*?"

I allowed a smile to grace my face. "Indeed, I would be most delighted."

And after offering good-byes, I departed for Fran's home.

A knock upon the door made me want to swoon, but I forced myself to remain vertical. I needed to be strong.

The door opened, and Mr. Fisk stood before me.

"Oh dear," I declared, not sure what I would say to the man whom I had most likely ruined.

"Hi, Polly," he said. "Come in."

Though I don't know how my feet moved forward,

they entered, and I found myself inside with Ruthie Carmichael sitting on the couch. Her wrists were free of the shackles of iron I had placed upon her. "Oh, dear," I declared once more.

Neither spoke, and I became even more disheartened. "I've come—" I faltered. "I've come to say sorry."

Mr. Fisk took a seat beside Miss Ruthie and grasped her hand in his. "We're listening, Polly." And the smile he offered encouraged me to proceed.

I coughed into my hand, willing the words to make their way from the depths of my heart to my mouth. "My dearest friends," I said, assuming a prostrate kneeling position with my head bowed low. "I am so very sorry," I said, recalling the events of that dreaded night. The weeping that overtook me could not be stopped. I pled for their forgiveness. "I am dreadfully sorry for the pain that I have caused you. Miss Carmichael, I beseech you to forgive me for calling the police and having you arrested. I hope this will not reflect badly on the Fisks, who have loved me since I was young. I was not in the right."

Ruthie smiled and placed her hand on my head, which I felt to be a very elegant gesture indeed. "It's all right. And actually, it's nice to know that George and Fran have such a concerned and caring friend, though I wish I didn't have to be arrested to find that out."

I grasped her hand in mine at her act of forgiveness. "And dear Mr. Fisk, you who have loved me like one of your own; you who forgave me when I almost got you killed at the hands of Miss Penny's suitor. Please forgive me. I haven't been very considerate of you or Fran and I've tried to control things as if you were in a book. I'll never do anything like that again, I assure you."

Mr. Fisk smiled very gently, which brought fresh tears to my eyes. "Well, Polly. Things did get quite out of hand. Thanks for apologizing. I know you've learned your lesson. Just leave the romance stuff to me. I still have a few tricks up my sleeve, even if I do work on computers."

"Indeed, I resign myself to this fate. No, even more so. I am convinced of this fate," I said.

Silence fell between us at the question that lingered on my tongue, but I could not utter it in fear I would cry once more.

Mr. Fisk seemed to sense this and shook his head. "She's not here, Polly. Sorry."

My heart was wrenched in two.

She did not wish to see me, and I could not blame her.

With a dejected heart I arose from my knees and bade them good-bye. "Thank you for bringing relief to a troubled mind and a burdened soul."

"Polly?" Mr. Fisk called out after me. "If you want to come back around dinner, she should be here."

"Thank you with all of my heart, dear Mr. Fisk. Though I do not expect my apology to be accepted, I know that I, indeed, must give it if I am to find any more rest in this life or the next."

And at that, I left the home of my once dearest and closest of friends and sought refuge in the Haven of Heaven. Perhaps the breeze flitting through the leaves and sounds of birds chirruping their delight in summer's warmth would soothe my tormented heart.

It was true, I had been forgiven by my sister and pardoned by Mr. Fisk and Miss Carmichael, but knowing that my bosom friend was perhaps lost to me forever was a thought that brought tears to my eyes and a bleeding wound to my heart.

I reached the Haven of Heaven, which was in beautiful bloom. The bright green of the leaves and the blossoming flowers that scented the air were indeed nourishing, though they could not fully take away my inward turmoil.

And that is when I saw her.

Fran! My bosom friend!

She sat beneath the shade of the Old One, twisting and pulling the embroidery thread on the start of a new bracelet. I stopped, wondering what to do.

Though words and thoughts had never been hard for me to find, in this instance I was speechless.

I did not want to scare her away, but I needed to speak with her. And so I willed my legs to move me forward.

"Hi," I said in a whisper not much louder than the leaves brushing together in the wind.

She looked up, her face blank of all emotion, and then stood. "Hi."

"Please don't run away yet," I pleaded, for it looked like she was about to dart off.

She sighed. "Do you know what you almost did? I mean, Polly Madassa, you almost ruined my entire life. And even besides the whole 'get my best friend's father's girlfriend in jail' thing, you've been just a plain old lousy friend! You never listen to a thing I say and you have no idea what it feels like to have not had a mom. And . . . ugh."

I began to cry at that point, remembering how I'd acted toward her and how I'd treated her and her father. Knowing that being without a mother had been so agonizing for her crushed me deeply... knowing I had not listened well to her as a bosom friend was pain my heart could not bear. "I know," I sobbed. "I was kinda treating you and your dad like... like the characters in the books I love so much."

She placed her hands on her hips. "Kind of, Polly?"

"Okay." I sniffed. "I was treating you that way. And I'm sorry about not listening and for thinking I understood and could fix things when I don't understand and I just can't fix things to how I want them." I covered my face with my hands, sat, and leaned back against the Old One. "I'm a wretched, horrid friend. I'm so very sorry for what I have done and the pain I have caused you." She sat beside me, picking at the green grass around us. "So, whether or not you can continue to be my friend, please say that perhaps in the future there might be a chance that I will be forgiven by you."

We sat in silence, each moment making that forgiveness seem more and more impossible.

She turned to me. "All right, Polly. I'll forgive you—"

"Really?! Oh, Fran—"

She held up her hand to silence me, and I quickly closed my mouth. "But, there are a few conditions."

"Anything, dearest friend. Name it and I shall perform it. Remaining bosom friends is all that I—"

"One," she stated, cutting off my sentence. "You have to promise that you'll try really hard to listen and not just talk all the time."

"Consider it done, my dearest friend."

"Two. No more matchmaking."

"But Fran, I'm not quite sure," I began. "Perhaps this is not the course I could devote my life to, but indeed I—" I stopped at once, noticing her eyes narrowing at me with a very menacing look. "I will matchmake no longer."

"And three. You've got to swear, promise, vow... whatever, that you will not get in the way of my dad and Ruthie."

"I promise," I declared, grabbing a lock of my hair. "Do you wish me to seal my vow with one of my silky tresses?"

She rolled her eyes. "No, Polly. I don't. And the word is *hair*, not *tresses*."

"Oh, but Fran, *tresses* is so much more romantic. Don't you think?"

"Not really," Fran said, once again resuming her bracelet-making.

I nodded. "Yes, Fran. I can see that we are strangers living side by side," I said, repeating one of my favorite lines from *Anne of Green Gables.* "But not in a bad way, right?"

Fran wrapped her arm around my shoulders and hugged me to her. "No, not in a bad way at all."

I took up a bundle of embroidery thread so that I might make a bracelet alongside her. "Beloved friends forever?" I asked, feeling the weight of my iniquities lifting off my burdened shoulders.

"Yep, best friends forever."

As dusk settled upon my bedroom and enveloped me in a romantic glow from my open window, I picked up the piece of stationery that had led me on this journey of love and discovery. "Love in the Making," I read aloud, and sighed.

Indeed, love was not a book and I had seen it manifest in ways I had not dreamt, but still it had mysteriously come just the same. And with that I was greatly pleased.

Besides, it had gotten me into quite a lot of trouble and had hurt those whom I loved most.

It was not worth it in the least.

And so I took up the paper, folded it neatly in half, and placed it in a small wooden box I kept hidden under a loose wooden plank on the floor.

Having it too near would only serve as a temptation, I feared, but I did not wish to burn it, for it also reminded me to never, ever go down that path again.

Once I placed the floorboard back into place, I sat upon my bed and breathed deeply the salty breeze that lifted my curtains with its delicate hands.

And then, leaning against my bed, I took up *Jane Eyre*, and got lost at once in the noble woman's life and in the stormy eyes of her lover, Mr. Rochester.

Epilogue:

In Which I End My Tale

Fran clanked her spoon against the side of her crystal glass, and I did the same, gazing upon Mr. Nightquist and his bride as they kissed each other lightly upon the lips.

Charles's manners had not improved much. He was now using the reception area as a racetrack and poor Melissa Anne was on her fifth or sixth lap around.

I tore my eyes away from them, trying to bring my mind to a more pleasant place. "I hope that my husband has lips the color of a pink grapefruit," I said, imagining my own dear Bradley, who was at that moment filling up a goblet with punch for my refreshment. Indeed, he was quite a gentleman. We had spoken quite often since that night when he and Mr. Nightquist pulled me from the sea. He had even escorted me to dinner one night, and under candlelight we shared a most delicious cheese pizza. "Indeed, I would absolutely adore a man whose lips were the color of a grapefruit. Wouldn't you?"

Fran knocked me in the shoulder. "Maybe, but not if he tasted like a grapefruit, right?"

"Of course not, Fran. That would be absurd." She laughed and I gazed about the room, drinking in the sights and sounds around me.

My mother and father swayed back and forth next to Mr. Fisk and Ruthie Carmichael on the dance floor. Clementine was wrapped in the arms of her newest beau and . . . what was this?

I noticed a dashing young gentleman standing next to Bradley by the refreshment table and eyeing Fran in her lavender dress. Though she had forbidden me to work my romantic magic on another person, and I too had renounced "love in the making," I had been overcome the past week after finding the perfect date for Mrs. Miller, the lonely piano teacher. He was a well-bred real estate agent who frequented the bakery and in whose arms she was now locked in embrace.

I had also aided Clint, who was now happily in the arms of a girl named Sophia. And Edward was with Tracy—the girl who had stolen his heart from the first. But my greatest wish by far was for my dearest friend. Yet there were not many suitors who were worthy of her.

But this young man, he was surely a vision who would bring my bosom friend the same joy that I felt with my dearest Bradley.

"You know," I said to Fran, gesturing to the suitor, "that young man has been unable to take his eyes off your delicate beauty. I fear that he is much in love with you. Leave it to me, my dearest. I will have the two of you conversing and bonding within moments." I had gotten up and started toward the gentleman when I was suddenly grasped from behind.

"Oh, no you don't. You promised me. That"—she pointed to Jack the Nipper, tied to a chair leg by a short red leash—"is the only kind of romance you are allowed to arrange, got it?"

I laughed and studied the little dog. "Yes, you are right, my dearest friend. And I noticed a beautiful dachshund just this morning trotting by the bakery. Still, he is a very handsome boy indeed."

"No, Polly. If I want to talk to him, I will."

I nodded. "Very well, I wash my hands of the subject."

"Good," Fran said. "Now try to think of a doggie

friend for Jack. That should keep you busy for the rest of the year."

"Yes, about that dachshund, do you think she would like a scone or a croissant? Really, I want to give the dachshund a good impression of Jack, since he does have abundant faults."

Fran laughed, her face bursting with red, and I couldn't help but join in her laughter, though really, the thought plagued me throughout the rest of the evening. When I got home I wrote up, in my best calligraphy, a plan to unite the canines.

And settled on a scone.

acknowledgments

Just as a fine, deliciously baked pastry has many ingredients, so did this story have many ingredients as it was measured, mixed, rolled, and baked into the book you hold in your hands.

To my wonderful, amazing agent, Rebecca Sherman, who took a chance on me and made my writing—and therefore, this book—ten times better than I thought it could be.

To my editor, Elizabeth Law, who understood Polly so perfectly and who asked all the right questions, and laughed at all the right parts.

To the entire Egmont USA family: Doug Pocock and

Regina Griffin, for a wonderful steak dinner and welcoming me with so much kindness. To Mary Albi, Alison Weiss, Nico Medina, Greg Ferguson, Rob Guzman, and Jeanine Henderson. I am one girl who knows how very lucky she is.

To my online critique mates who first read Polly's elaborate story and who thought she was funny and endearing enough to reread over and over again. The Cudas: Lisa Amowitz, Cyndy Henzel, Cathy Giordiano, Kate Chell Milford, Dhonielle Clayton, and Linda Acorn. And Elitecritiquers: Jean Reidy, Shannon Caster, Julie M. Prince, Lauren Whitney, and David Macinnis Gill. You all are more amazing than I can ever say. Thank you for your praise, your honesty, and your friendship.

To my fifth-grade teacher, Mrs. Jan Baughman, who believed in my first story about a lion named Walop. Wherever you are in the world, thank you!

To my close friends here in Colorado who make me laugh, cry, and who have allowed me to become a part of their lives, their families, and their stories. Phil and Anne Gallagher, Kent and Melissa Gledhill, Kirk and

Sarah Livesay, Chris Gygi, Jen Morgan, and Bruce and Katie Buller. And to Audrey Buller, who first gave Polly her voice. I love you all!

To my parents, Chris and Wendy Devlin. Words cannot ever tell the world enough of what you gave me and continue to give me each day. I hardly consider you as my parents now. You are so much more than that. Thank you for always believing I could do it, even in fifth grade. I love you both so very much.

To my older sister Alisa, who is the real writer and artist. Thanks for letting me tag along with you when we were little and look up to you now that we're real, live grown-ups. You are a barrel of fun.

Those who know me best know that, above all else, I love to laugh. And therefore one of the people I love above all else is my younger sister Suzanne. You are my kindred spirit, my bosom friend!

To Gracie, Isaac, Ella Jane, and Noah. Thank you for every single moment with you. I love you with a ferocious and undying love!

And to John, always to John. You make my heart beat faster.